Evolution Eye Floater

by James L. Steele

Published by KTM Publishing

Print edition set in Fanwood, a royalty-free typeface.

Print edition ISBN: 978-1-7373899-1-0

I

Barry woke up to the sound of a tiny, charismatic voice.

> "Comrades! The light will return soon, and all deeds that were once secret will be brought out into the open! Come, comrades! Gather all! We seek the RETURN OF THE LIGHT!"

Muffled cheers and amens filled one side of Barry's head.

> "DO YOU WANT TO SEE THE LIGHT!? Do you clamor for illumination?! Do you seek the light?!"

More muffled amens and cheering. Barry felt tidal forces swirling around in his right eyeball. He clenched his eyelids even tighter, as if that would help him shut out the noise, and tried to go back to sleep.

> "The light shows us who we are! It shows us what we're made of! It shows us the way things really are, not the way they seem to be! The light!"
>
> "THE LIGHT!"

The amens grew in volume, and the waves in Barry's eyeball became so extreme he felt it shifting in its socket.

"THE *LIGHT*!"

The amenning and cheering and swirling had so much force Barry thought his eye would burst from his skull.

"SHOW US THE LIGHT!
SHOW US WHO WE ARE!
SHOW US! WE BESEECH
THE LIGHT TO RETURN
AND SHINE UPON US!
SHINE!"

After each successive refrain, Barry saw fireworks flashes and sparks in his right eye.

"SHINE!"

flash

"SHINE!"

flash spark

"WE NEED THE LIGHT,
SO SHINE!"

flash

"SHINE!"

FLASH SPARK

"SHINE!"

*SPARKSPARKFLASH-
FLASHFLASH*

"Shine on us, oh light!"

The flashing and sparking on his vision was too bright to ignore. He opened his eyes to the morning sun coming through his window.

"The light! It has returned!"

The flashes and sparking and amenning and cheering went off like a disco drug trip. Barry tried to see, but floaters blocked the vision in his right eye. They had gathered in the center, facing the outside, basking in the morning light, cheering and swirling around and jumping up and down on his retina.

"Thank you, o light! We give our thanks! We give our utmost thanks to you!"

The flashes were like punches to the gut. Barry braced himself and shook his head around. His eye floaters swirled helplessly. The revival congregation quickly degenerated into squeals of ecstasy like preschoolers on a roller coaster.

Barry gyrated for a solid minute, making sure his eye floaters were completely mixed around. Like shuffling a new deck of cards, he had to do it several times to make sure they were randomized, otherwise they would regroup.

Thoroughly dizzy, Barry looked out the window. His eye floaters were just that now. Random lines and specks in his vision harmlessly floating in the vitreous humor. The preaching stopped, and so had the celebration. Barry caught a glimpse of the charismatic one drifting with the rest of them.

He pulled his focus inward and checked the floaters in his left eye. They were dormant, silent, delighted in the joy of being caught up in the motion, as usual. It was still difficult to see through the thick soup of webbed sticks, but at least they were quiet and content to drift. Unlike the rebellious floaters in his right eye, the ones in the left were non-sentient, just as they should be.

Barry waited a few minutes for the dizziness to pass, and then he rolled out of bed and walked to the dresser. He strained to see through his floaters as he opened the drawer and pulled out the shirt. He'd been doing it for years, and he thought he'd be used to it by now, but they were always in the way. So many of them, floating around, basking in fluidic motion and light.

He hated having to make a conscious effort to see beyond what was inside his eyeball. It was annoying, like becoming conscious of breathing, thinking about every inhale and exhale. Barry tried to lose himself in routine and allow his vision sink into his subconscious. He slipped on his underwear and then his cotton slacks.

Barry's suits cost him almost as much as his house. He would have been happy for cheap imitations, but the Attire Auditor routinely wandered the building, reading shirt labels, pants tags, and sock monograms for authenticity like an appraiser on the *Antiques Road Show*. He'd know if Barry were wearing a knockoff, and he'd be fired for failing to keep up appearances. Company policy stated that all employees must represent the company while in the building, and that meant he had to look like a million Platcoins at all times.

Barry grabbed a necktie and walked to the bathroom. He faced himself in the mirror and began the ritual of securing it. His vision had just reached beyond his eyeball when suddenly a small clump of floaters obscured the vision. The clump quickly became an opaque ball as every floater in his right eye gathered in the middle and stared out through the pupil. While Barry tied the silk fabric, he heard soft voices rise:

"Light..."

"It's the light."

"It shows us—"

Barry didn't give them the chance. He flicked his head a couple times, breaking up the crowd and swirling it around his eyeball. Barry waited for his vision to stabilize and resumed looping the silk fabric over and under and around and through until finally he had a perfect necktie. He let his arms drop to his sides and stood up straight.

This suit made Barry look so professional his own mother called him sir, not out of love, but fear. Barry smiled at himself, as he did every morning. He looked like a million Platcoins, felt like a million Platcoins... If only he *had* a million Platcoins.

Barry walked to the bathroom scale. He waited a few seconds for the machine to measure his weight. 415 Platform Weight Units. Barry sighed. He wished there were something he could do to get thin.

He left the bathroom and returned to his bedroom. He picked up his phone and tapped the Platform app. He updated his status to *awake*.

Platform informed him that, based on his previous meals, he would certainly enjoy the meal it had just ordered for him and was en route right now.

Seconds later, Barry's doorbell rang. He fetched the delivery, eager to see what Platform had ordered for him.

He waited until he sat down at the kitchen table before opening the boxes, warm and steaming and filling the room with deep-fried goodness.

His phone pinged, indicating it was time for his breakfast selfie. He took one while he opened his first box: a deep-fried egg sandwich with a side of french toast topped with liquid Captain Crunch. He then took a selfie trying the drink that came with his breakfast. Barry didn't have to fake being surprised by the coffee-flavored ice cream shake.

He made sure to give thanks for this sponsored breakfast.

Platform always knew what he wanted, and when he wanted it.

After satisfying his morning selfie quota, Barry carried the whole ensemble to the living room. He sat down on a very rectangular couch as the walls switched on, surrounding him with his Platform feed. The algorithm selected the local news stream for him this morning, as it had for years. Barry's teeth squished through the layers of grease in his egg sandwich.

"Sir," said the reporter on screen, "can you tell us in your own words what you witnessed at this time shareholders bottom line diversity process."

The man in front of the camera was white and at least 440 Platform Weight Units, eyes vacant. He was just lowering his cell phone after updating his Platform status to *streaming*. "Well I was in line to pay for coffee when you know this guy... uh... yeah."

A very brief pause, and then the man raised his cell phone and started tapping it, updating his status again. The camera turned and focused on the reporter.

"A shocking development overnight."

The news returned to the anchor, who directed the focus to another knifing that happened last night. A different reporter interviewed an eyewitness on the scene.

"Ma'am, please give us some insight into what happened at this time, and how you felt."

The woman on camera was also very white and looked about 360 PWUs. "I was pumping gas and heard a scream from inside. It was loud..."

Having reached her character limit, she trailed off, the thought simply too large for her brain to hold without being trained in the techniques of speaking outside one's limit.

Her mouth hung open for several seconds. No sound came out until she muttered, "Uh... yeah."

Then she looked down at her cell phone and started typing on it. On the left wall, Barry's Platform feed showed him suggested posts from this woman. She had taken her routine selfies with her sponsored breakfast as well: deep-fried corn flakes suspended in a bowl of maple-flavored syrup. Barry gave the pictures a *like*, but did not follow her, as that could be construed as stalking.

Barry's vision refocused on his eyeball. Floaters had been drawn to the changing light patterns caused by the stream. They had gathered to watch, and the cobweb ball they formed blocked the smartwall. Barry shook his head lightly and broke it up. He stared through the swirling lines and clumps as commercials began airing.

Barry finished his sponsored breakfast. He posted an update and a review, using one of his selfies.

Meal from @FastBrekk. Needed a good day. Thx for the cereal!

Sixty characters exactly, so no need to augment with businessspeak. Platform's interface didn't allow for that anyway. All forms of expression could be contained in sixty characters, so it was never any trouble to stay within Platform's maximum limit. There was never anything else to say. Only Barry's job required him to go beyond.

He got up and walked to the front door. Platform knew he did so at this moment in the morning, so it turned off the walls and dimmed the lights while Barry grabbed his keys and wallet from an end table. Platform locked the front door behind him, and he waddled down the short path from his front door to his driveway.

His car was expensive, but Platform had steered him toward a preowned offering, so it didn't break his bank while still passing the Vehicular Auditor, who checked his car daily to make sure it was still up to code. It always was because it was a successful man's car, therefore anyone who owned one must be successful. Barry tried to convince himself of this every day, and much like getting his right eye to focus beyond his floaters, he eventually got lost in routine and believed it for exactly nine hours a day.

He updated his Platform status to *driving*. Platform immediately interfaced with his car and backed him out of the driveway. Platform knew his route and aimed the vehicle in the direction of the office in downtown. His car accelerated for five seconds before bumping up against the tail end of traffic.

Barry updated his Platform status to *red light again lol*.

Barry's car never got above 15 Platform Distance Units per hour the whole commute due to the stoplights. The first light lasted ten minutes, and then finally the car in front of him moved forward. Barry updated his Platform status to *green light*. Twelve cylinders gunned it for three seconds before screeching to a stop.

red light lol

Eighty people gave his status various reactions, including grouchy faces and thumbs up and champagne glasses.

His daily commute crossed just twenty city blocks but lasted over an hour. Barry once considered walking, but that was too inconvenient at his weight. Plus, the Vehicular Auditor would notice he didn't bring his car to work and cite him; company policy stated that true professionals always drove, so he made sure to fight traffic every day like a professional.

The light turned green. Upon updating his Platform status, Barry's car zoomed through the intersection and slammed on the brakes, screeching to a stop behind a line of cars at the next red light. He looked at the sights. An elderly woman was on her cell phone, talking to someone.

"I'm not sure what's wrong I just forgot again I swear I left..." She hit her character limit, paused, lost what she was saying, and continued. "Well, you know what I'm saying, dear."

Barry looked to his other side. A young man on the phone. "No, I'm not breaking up with you Lisa I'm just sayin we should... uh... yeah..."

The man listened, nodding vigorously.

"Lisa, Lisa don't worry I wasn't with anyone else I swear you... uh... yeah." He paused for a few seconds, then said, "Well, you know what I'm sayin, don't you?"

"Proles," Barry said, smiling. "At the mercy of their character limit."

He said it at least twice a day to remind himself that he wasn't one of them anymore. He had moved up in the world. He was a professional.

Green light. Barry's car zoomed through the intersection and screeched to a stop at the next light. He listened to the proles to pass the time. On the way he passed four Flui-X-Change stations advertising their bundle of the week: free oil change for your car with purchase of blood transfusion.

Barry checked those signs every day, but they never advertised what he really needed. He had been waiting for them to offer a bundle deal on eye fluid for the past four years, but it was always blood, or lymph, or insulin, or bile. All the designer fluids everyone heard of and knew were essential to survival.

While he gawked at the average person and wistfully wished for a deal, the floaters in his right eye collected into a big cobweb ball and started slamming against his retina. Three bright flashes of light hit him in less than a second. Barry reeled from the shock.

He smacked his right temple with his palm. A few of the floaters separated from the ball and drifted in carefree glee. The remaining held each other and bounced from one side of Barry's eye to the other, sending bright flashes directly into Barry's brain.

Barry grabbed the steering wheel and threw his head around and around and side to side, whipping in every direction as hard as he could without breaking his neck. After a minute, his eye fluid was swirling so fast he couldn't even see the floaters, just a greyish-brown soup. Eventually it slowed, and Barry now saw the cobwebs and bent rods of his eye floaters twisting and turning in every direction, happily caught up in the current.

Barry heard horns honking at him. He looked up. The light was green, and it changed to yellow. He updated his status, but it was too late. The light changed to red. The vehicle's safety systems screeched it to a halt. He then received a notice from his insurance company that Platform had reported this incident of distracted driving and would increase his premium by 2%. His Platform feed became flooded with ads for competing auto insurance companies promising up to 3 forgivenesses per month before increasing his rate.

Barry punched the passenger seat, cursing not only for that but for being one light behind schedule.

Nobody cared about eye fluid. Nobody ever did a promotion that included a discount on an eye fluid exchange. As Barry had learned over the years, let any piece of body maintenance go too long, it becomes a crisis.

2

His office was small, but it was not a cubicle, so it was a step up. The rear wall had a window that extended from floor to ceiling. A large desk dominated the interior, matching executive chair facing the door, and two smaller chairs on the other side. Not a single person had ever sat in those chairs. The pen holder on top of the desk contained no pens, and he rarely turned on the computer.

Barry walked to his desk and leaned his empty briefcase against one of the legs. He sat down, stretched, took a deep breath, and updated his Platform status to *at work*. Platform interfaced with the security software in his office, and unlocked the top drawer, which held one thing: a tablet computer. He unplugged it from its charger built into the desk and waited patiently for it to wake up.

Barry didn't need a tablet to do his job. In years past he got by just fine with pen and paper, but then he was told the need to use pen and paper created a conflict of interest and invited corruption.

The welcome screen glowed in Barry's face. The floaters in his right eye started bunching up to bask in the light, which is why the camera only scanned his left eye to verify his identity to log him in.

The company took no chances with security in Barry's job position. It was important to ensure the integrity of the numbers Barry collected every day. There could be no risk of tampering or error. Any trends Barry recorded could cost the company millions of Platcoins in overhead.

Now ready to begin the day, Barry faced his blank computer monitor. He adjusted his tie and straightened his suit. He rose from the seat, tablet before him, and walked to the door.

First on his list of random offices to audit took him to floor number 6, beginning with cubicle 16. Barry rode the elevator alone for fifteen seconds. It stopped at floor 6, and Barry stepped into a maze of cubicles split down the center by one walkway, with the floor manager's office at the end. At cubicle 16, Barry scanned the barcode underneath the nameplate, and stepped inside.

"Pen and paperclip audit," Barry announced.

The hapless employee turned around in his office chair. The chair squeaked and strained to swivel 380 PWUs of single-white-male 180 degrees. Barry smelled stale salt coming through midnight fresh scent —the classic smell of sweat breaking through antiperspirant. It reminded Barry how much people in the office feared the auditors, and that he really had moved up.

The employee opened his drawer and showed him the pens and paperclips in his possession. Each had a unique barcode, and Barry scanned them one by one. The cube-dweller then showed Barry several stacks of paper, each with a paperclip in use. Barry changed the mode to "in use" and then scanned each of these paperclips. The employee had one pen in his shirt pocket, and Barry scanned it "in use" as well.

Barry then closed the cubicle in the computer, which showed all pens and paperclips accounted for. Barry smiled at the employee. Robbie was his name. Robbie Followercount. He'd known Robbie for years, since before he was P&P auditor. They hadn't really been friends since Barry's promotion, but Barry expected it. Friendships within the company would only create conflicts of interest, so Barry had to avoid human association.

"Excellent, Mr. Followercount," Barry said. "Your numbers always check out."

"Thank you sir I'm glad for your feedback it really helps me develop as... an..."

Robbie had been practicing his businessspeak as a means to extend his character limit, but he couldn't go too far above it before losing the thought. Barry still liked the guy. He smiled and clapped Robbie on the shoulder.

"At this time, you're welcome, Mr. Followercount," he said.

Robbie was about to turn around, but his gaze focused behind Barry. Standing behind him was the Staple and Paper Auditor, Jennifer Likeandsubscribe. Behind her was Jim, the Attire Auditor. Behind him stood Jeff, the Light Consumption Auditor.

Barry nodded to each of them as he walked by. Poor Robbie, Barry thought. Half the company's random audits started with him every day because Robbie's numbers were always good, which in turn made

Barry's superiors in the corporate office look good. Robbie would have at least an hour of audits before his work could even begin.

Barry walked the office floor, scanning pens and paperclips, noting which were "in use" and which were "dormant." The daily list always took him to random cubicles so there could be no attempt to recover lost supplies in preparation.

It took Barry an hour to audit the offices on this floor, and then he waddled to the elevator and rode it down. His eye floaters had been regrouping the whole time he audited floor six. Barry dared not shake his head in full view of the the Appearances and Actions auditor. Any action that made him seem less like a professional would be documented and could result in corrective action leading up to and including but not exceeding termination.

Alone in the elevator, Barry took a few moments to breathe naturally while one of the floaters was speaking

> "Light... It's beautiful. It's so beautiful. But... Where does it come from?"

This got everyone murmuring. Barry listened, too. It wasn't the charismatic one. This was someone different. Someone new.

> "Doesn't it make you wonder, comrades? Why does the light come and go?"

He shook his head. The floaters didn't break up the first time. They clung to each other in a tight ball and held on for dear life.

Barry braced himself against the elevator wall and threw his head around. By the time the doors opened, Barry looked composed and professional again, and the floaters drifted freely and mindlessly, as they should.

Barry walked from cubicle to cubicle as if he wasn't dizzy, inspecting random employees. The whole time his eye floaters regrouped and basked. Barry was in one young woman's cubicle scanning her paperclips when the preaching started.

"I want you all to remember the dark times."

The floaters in attendance gasped.

"Did I shock you?" opined the charismatic one. "Oh, what's that you say, we're not supposed to talk about the dark times when it's still light? Well, comrades, the time has come to face it. We know the light will leave us for a while and then return, and it will be up to us to bring it back."

Barry scanned the paperclips a little faster while the employee looked on, braced between her chair and her desk, trying not to appear scared for her life.

"We need the light, we thrive in its glory, and yet it deserts us. When it does, we tend to act in unspeakable ways. We do things to each other we would never do

in the presence of the light!
Why?"

Barry quickly closed out her cubicle and walked out to the aisle. He looked left and right and over both shoulders.

"Because we are wicked be-ings! Without the light, we are evil and vile creatures!"

He saw her. Alexis. The A&A auditor. She glanced at him from the corner of her eye, tapping on her tablet. Barry waved to her, smiling and pushing his focus out of his eyeball and into the outside world. He walked to the next cubicle and scanned the barcode.

"We must keep the light upon us at all times! The good times will last forever if we con-tinue to appeal to the light, but I ask then why does it leave at all? It leaves because of us, comrades! Because it knows we are wicked and vile! Our first experiment in bringing the light back was a suc-cess. It proves that the light needs us to appeal to it. We must entice the light to return and shine its glory down on us wicked things!"

Barry worked as fast as possible, speaking to peo-ple in the office as if the charismatic one weren't preaching in his ear while its congregation blocked the center of his vision. He'd gotten good at keeping him-self composed under these circumstances. Or at least he thought he was good at it; the charismatic one's preaching had been easy to tune out for months, but today it was speaking far in excess of Barry's character limit. They had never gone beyond sixty characters of information before, and the new development made Barry nervous.

At last the floor was complete, and he speed-walked to the elevator. He almost broke into a sweat in spite of the air conditioned office. He stepped onto an empty car, and as soon as the doors closed Barry thrashed around and sent his eye floaters swirling.

They used to go mindless and feral for days, but in recent months he could barely go an hour before they started regrouping. Five years ago, Barry could go an entire week before he had to break them up. It was becoming more and more difficult to make it through the day when every floor became a race to stay ahead of his eye floaters' rallies.

He moved to floor 3. Then 4. Then 5, struggling to keep his composure the whole while. He was sure the A&A auditor was on to him. Barry saw Alexis on three out of the six floors, and he was beginning to suspect she suspected something was wrong with him, but Barry never lost his poise, never worked himself up to a sweat, never behaved in any way that could be misconstrued as unprofessional.

His daily audit routine now complete, Barry rode the elevator to his office. Six other people rode with him, so he had to wait before breaking up his floaters this time.

Once on the top floor, he sat at his desk and uploaded the data to the central server. It took less than a minute to update and show Barry the overall results of the entire day's audit. He had found numerous discrepancies. In spite of these measures to control overhead office supply costs, some paperclips were not where they were supposed to be. Paperclips and pens were for each individual's use only. No transfer of ownership was permitted without Barry's written consent, and yet some paperclips were in the wrong cubicles, pens in the pockets of the wrong employees. Some were missing altogether.

Quickly Barry generated official transfer warning requests, ordering certain employees to exchange specific pens and paperclips. Others were written up for misuse of company property (which meant loss of a pen or a paperclip). Some were on their final warning, and another would lead to termination with the cost of the lost supplies and administration fees deducted from their severance pay.

It was now time for his lunch break, and right on schedule a delivery drone opened a hatch in the window and dropped off the meal Platform had ordered for Barry, using feedback from his previous five hundred and ratings to select exactly what Barry wanted: two pints of deep-fried ice cream and a cup of hot cream mixed with a dash of coffee on the side. He ate while working, shaking his head every few minutes to keep his floaters apart. Employees were not required to work through lunch, but if the sensors on his phone detected no hand movement for a certain amount of time, Platform sent an alert to his supervisor, and he would be at risk of being retroactively clocked out for the motionless period.

Barry continued typing reports and sending them to each floor manager. Barry knew these reports would print off automatically in each manager's office, and they would be distributed to the individual employees and filed in every employee's permanent record.

In addition, Barry knew, every other auditor in the building was generating these reports. Some people spent so much time keeping up with the auditor's reports they barely produced anything, but Barry and the other auditors like him were the solution to the most basic problems of every office, which made the whole process worthwhile.

The last three hours of Barry's work day were spent in random inspections fed to him through the tablet system. He gave each employee at least an hour to address any concerns he noted, and then he revisited those with misplaced, unaccounted, or unauthorized pens and paperclips.

While he was at it, he did surprise inspections of random employees, entering their new data, giving the company extra information on pen and paperclip use. Barry also had access to elaborate computer models tracking each pen and paperclip's movement through the office. He could see the patterns and identify trouble areas Barry needed to focus on, and he kept special tabs on everyone in such zones.

It would be easy work if not for the distractions within his eyeball. Again Barry raced to finish his inspections before his floaters became too organized so he could retreat to the elevator and break them up. His peers mistook this for work ethic. It made Barry look good on the A&A report.

Finally Barry returned the tablet to the desk charger, locked it, locked the office, and retreated to his car. He updated his Platform status to *off work*, and the car automatically drove him to a restaurant it knew he wanted based on his previous one hundred evening meals.

Once out of the drivethru at one of his favorite deep-fried hamburger chains, he updated his status to *commuteEating*. Platform drove his car into traffic and halted behind thirty cars waiting at a red light. Barry unwrapped a double-all-beef burger encased in pancake batter and deep fried to perfection. He ate dinner while stopped in traffic, as usual. Between bites, he enjoyed another ice cream shake, passion fruit today, just the fun flavor he craved after a day at work like today.

Delivery drones dropped meals to other cars. Barry sometimes opted for this, but it was cheaper to drive there and pick it up himself. Every single person in earshot marveled that Platform ordered exactly what they had in mind. Some even suspected it was reading their minds. It wasn't, rather using their previous thousand ratings to predict what they wanted now, thus it was never wrong.

Barry waited until he was three stoplights away from the office building before thrashing his head. When his vision straightened and he was sure the light was still red, he noticed the Flui-X-Change again. He wistfully observed a black woman of 400 Platform Weight Units receiving a routine blood transfusion while she waited for her oil change and tire rotation.

When he was a boy, his body filtered its own blood, produced its own insulin, lubricated its own joints, and excreted its own urine. But at age 6, when a person is 150 PWUs, the body's systems start to shut down. The problem had been so widespread it threatened to bring the country to a standstill, but Platform's dedicated team of experts proposed that technology could compensate for the natural decline of the body's systems. Other companies stepped in and offered the procedures on the go. Barry received his first blood change from Flui-X-Change on his sixth birthday, and he had been a loyal customer ever since.

Barry had been to that particular shop for all his routine bodily maintenance since his promotion: his blood transfusions, his urine purges, his bowel cleanings, his insulin replenishment. He even went there for the periodic maintenance: his bile changes, his lymph refills, his brain fluid balancing, his joint fluid refills. Expensive, but necessary if he wanted to continue living, which was the reason to have a job and a presence on Platform.

He knew the consequences—Platform influencers and news streams had drilled it into his mind since preschool: forget to change your blood at least once a month and you'll seize up in your sleep. Neglect to top off your lymph fluid and you'll develop an imbalance and your left side might swell up with water while your right side deflated. Neglect your joint lube and you'll turn into a surfboard within a year. Neglecting one's eye fluid was said to result in blindness due to the thick soup of floaters that would form. Nobody said anything about sentient creatures evolving. Eye fluid was the last thing anybody needed, and thus the most expensive.

Barry wanted to save up for the eye fluid exchange, but every time he got a little extra money something ate it up, like car maintenance, blood changes, joint lubrication, insurance, the sub-pump, a new suit he had to buy to avoid the Attire Auditor citing him for wearing the same clothes for too many consecutive months. In spite of his job status, he was still just barely making it.

He would normally just charge the procedure on a credit card, but all his cards were maxed out, and he was at the maximum credit limit for his income, according to his Platformscore™. He spent so much money maintaining his professional position he had no future money to borrow to pay for body maintenance.

As he thought this, his floaters jumped up and down on his retina. They had been doing this more and more often, sun dances to the light, trying to appease it, begging it not to leave them. They were holding a rave as the sun set. Barry was tired of making himself sick to keep them broken up. He let them dance for the whole duration of one red light. Finally the flashes became too painful, and he steeled himself and banged his head against the steering wheel.

Barry unwrapped the second deep friend double patty burger and picked up his second ice cream shake. Coffee flavored this time. Platform always knew exactly what he was in the mood for.

3

Barry jumped awake, clutching his head as if trying to keep his eyes in their sockets. His brain had lit up in white and yellow sparks timed to cries of—

> "LIGHT! LIGHT! Bring back the LIGHT! LIGHT! LIGHT"

Each unanimous shout raised a fireworks burst up his optic nerve and directly into his visual cortex. The floaters in his right eye were jumping up and down on his retina. Every part of it. He clenched his eyes shut. As the crowd chanted for a return of the light, a single voice spoke over the rhythm.

> "We beseech you to return! We ask for relief from the darkness and crave to feel the warmth. To feel the vision! To remember the past and see the future!"

> "LIGHT! LIGHT! Bring back the LIGHT!"

> "We crave it!"

> "LIGHT! LIGHT! Bring back the LIGHT!"

> "Return to us!"

The agony increased. The flashes pushed him out of bed and sent him tearing through the house like an animal trying to escape a thunderstorm. One flash overpowered Barry, sending him to the floor in the hallway, curling into fetal position while clenching his eyes. After five minutes, Barry couldn't take it anymore.

"STOP! STOP IT! SHUT UP! SHUT UP! SHUT UP!"

But his floaters kept going. Barry had tried to reason with them many times. They never heard him, no matter how much he pleaded. Barry didn't understand how his eye floaters learned Platformlish but didn't understand him.

The chanting rose. They slammed into his retina harder and harder, shoving brighter and brighter fireworks up his brain. Barry opened his eyes, resisting the instinct to keep them closed.

It was early in the morning, so no lights on. Barry lifted himself to his hands and knees and shook his head around for a solid minute. He stopped, letting himself feel dizzy. The fireworks continued and so did the chanting. Barry couldn't see them, but he figured they had interlocked limbs and were bracing against the retina so they couldn't be shaken around this time.

Barry leaned against the wall and slammed his head against it again and again in opposite time to their chanting, hoping to interrupt them just before they jumped. He did this twenty times just to be thorough, and then he knelt on the carpet in the hallway and waited.

The flashes only stopped for a few seconds. The chanting continued, and now the charismatic one's speech changed.

> "The swirl won't stop us now! We resist it! We call you, o light! We call upon you to return!"

"LIGHT! LIGHT!"

Barry dropped to his side, holding his head between both hands and twisting it in all directions as fast as he could.

"LIGHT! LIGHT!"

Barry lay on his back, forcing his eyes to stay open. They were jumping out of sync now, so instead of seeing one giant blast he was saw a thousand individual sparks. Barry cried.

"Please stop... Please..."

They didn't. They kept chanting, kept appealing, kept preaching.

Barry looked around from the floor. He strained to see through the fireworks and concentrate through the voices practically right next to his eardrum. After six flashes and twelve deafening cries for the light, Barry figured out where he was. He rolled over and crawled along the floor, panting through a throbbing headache as their cries became synchronized and the flashes intensified.

Barry reached up from the floor and picked up his phone. He changed his Platform status to *awake*. Instantly, light flooded the house.

Barry's eye floaters cheered. The jumping halted and Barry now saw that his floaters had indeed formed an elaborate lattice. They had interwoven their webby limbs into a structure meant to keep themselves anchored. With the return of the light, many of them had jumped from the retina and drifted around his eyes in absolute bliss.

Barry took his chance. He shook his head around and around, mixing his eye fluid up. The lattice came apart. The floaters separated and swirled. He was sure there were more of them now. He wished he knew where they came from.

The floaters lost themselves in the bliss of momentum. The fireworks stopped. His head was quiet again. Barry dropped and rolled to his back.

"Please let me sleep. Just let me sleep…"

This was the third time his floaters had woken him up tonight. As recently as a few months ago, Barry's eye floaters had been content to wait for daylight, but recently they had begun to take matters into their own hands. Barry wished he could explain how these things worked, but he didn't think they'd understand even if they could hear him.

After a few minutes, Barry closed his eyes again and tried to rest. The voice of the charismatic one woke him up. His floaters were gathering in the presence of the light. Barry could just make out the shadow they cast through the back of his eyelid.

> "Look before us! The light is there! We can see it! We can feel it! But something is blocking it! What is blocking it, my com-

> rades? We are! Yes, we are! Our wicked deeds in the darkness are keeping the light from us! We are the shadow, and the light cannot reach us now! We must turn from our wicked ways! We must increase our efforts! As long as the light never leaves, we will never be evil! We won't be compelled to do these evil things to one another!"

Amenning drifted through Barry's skull. Barry opened his eyes.

The floaters cheered. Barry saw them surrounding the charismatic one in the center of an intricate ball of webbed limbs. Barry shook his head. They weren't prepared this time. Their revival broke up easily, and the entire congregation swirled helplessly, going silent as they lost themselves in the current.

Barry took the moment to check his other eye. Dormant floaters. Numerous and blocking his vision, but they didn't seem to be moving on their own at all. Barry was glad for his left eye. He wouldn't know what to do if he had to deal with two congregations at once. Bad enough the charismatic one's speeches made less and less sense. Barry wondered how it had learned to speak beyond its character limit.

He looked out the window and noticed daylight. He had slept maybe a total of three hours. Barry clutched his head and rose from the carpet. He shuffled to the front door and picked up the breakfast delivery Platform had selected for him. He could smell it: a three-pack of deep-fried breakfast sandwiches with a side of cinnamon-sugar pizza. Citrus soda syrup as a beverage, undiluted, as regular soda ceased to be sweet enough for him by age 10. Just the kind of feel-good breakfast he needed.

Barry groaned and waited for his depth of field to extend beyond his right eyeball.

4

Barry sat at the rectangular table along with ten other people. He couldn't remember the last time management felt the need to call a meeting of the auditors before.

He was nervous, but he was sure not to let it show, lest the A&A auditor note the unprofessional action in her log. Barry also tried to keep his sweating to a minimum or Dale, the Water Consumption Auditor, would note that in his report and put him on notice as likely to make an extra trip to the water fountain. The last thing Barry needed was a citation on his perfect record.

Barry noticed every auditor making a conscious effort to hold in their sweat while they waited in silence. No one dared make conversation to fill it for fear that Bob, the Air and Conversation Auditor, would note the misuse of the company's air for personal recreation in his report. Everyone breathed regularly, evenly, in unison.

After three hours in strained silence and synchronized breathing and agonizing sweat retention, someone finally walked in. Barry didn't recognize this 390-PWU man, and following close behind him came a line of fifty men and women marching nose to neck, each no lighter than 360 Platform Weight Units. They took ten minutes to file into the room and take positions along the wall. They made no conversation. They took in no more air than absolutely necessary.

They were tagalongs. This meant the 390-PWU man entering the room was a Big Boss™. It was part of conforming to Appearances and Actions standards: all Big Bosses needed tagalongs in order to project an air of importance around them. This Big Boss had so many tagalongs they occupied the entire perimeter of the meeting room, squeezing in on the auditors seated around the table.

They breathed in unison. They blinked in unison. Their one eye that faced the center of the meeting room strained to make peripheral vision into forward vision. A few of the more experienced tagalongs had fully evolved eyeballs on the sides of their heads.

Future Big Bosses in training, Barry thought. Only the strongest would survive Management Culling™.

When everyone had a place and the door closed, the Big Boss stood at one end of the table just out of reach of the tagalongs, who were slurping the air trying to taste his essence in order to gain an advantage at the next Company Death Trial™.

"Ladies and gentlemen," said the Big Boss. "Thank you all for attending this meeting. I promise to make it short. Your time is valuable, just as my time is, just as the company's time is. On that note, that's why I called this meeting today, at this time."

Barry almost fidgeted, but he stopped himself, glancing sideways at the A&A auditor. Alexis glared at Barry. He tried to stare at her, but his floaters obscured her facial features and he couldn't make out if there was any suspicion in her eyes.

"Ma'am," said the Big Boss, gesturing to Alexis. "I wish to engage you in a dialogue at this time regarding your documented roles within the company as part of my effort to familiarize myself with such a diverse group at this time."

She turned from Barry and faced the Big Boss. "Alexis Sponsoredcontent. My core role is to audit the appearances and actions of employees, noting any behavior or demeanor that might impact the company in a negative way according to established process leading to the creation of shareholder value."

"Very good. And... you, sir, what is your function in the company?"

He had gestured at Simon, the Tape and Memory Auditor. Simon waited until his allocated moment to exhale, and then spoke evenly.

"Simon Termsandconditions. My core role in the company is to track tape usage and observe patterns and trends of potential waste that would negatively impact company overhead. I strive to proactively do the same for computer memory as well."

"Thanks," said the Big Boss.

Barry wondered if the boss noticed each person was trying to outdo the previous speaker in how professional he could respond. The surest way to prove one deserved his or her high-paying position as a professional was to show one's prowess in businessspeak—that one was capable of speaking beyond the mind's natural limit of sixty characters. Barry hoped he wouldn't have to go last.

"And... you," said the Big Boss, "if you would, what is your job at this time?"

Corey, the Marker and Post It Auditor, spoke in time with his required moments of breath. "I'm Corey Doingnumbers. My core roles, at this time, include tracking marker and Post-It notes to proactively search for trends of waste that may have a negative impact on the company's bottom line, at this time, shareholders, marginal, proactive, today."

Barry felt like hiding in the subatomic realm. His eye floaters danced in the light of the fluorescents above. On that thought, the Big Boss called Jeff next.

"I am Jeff Banneduser. My job designation, at this current point in current time, today, is Light Consumption Auditor, proactively. I seek to understand, through my unique communication style, how an individual employee, at this time, consumes light, and follow flowcharts to ascertain in real time how much light is actually needed for each employee to achieve his or her diverse task at hand. Proactively."

Around they went. They heard from the Printer and Ink Auditor. Then from the Air and Conversation Auditor, Bob. Each job description got longer and longer, each employee obligated to use more words than the last.

"And last, you, sir," said the Big Boss. "What is your job at this time?"

A single drop of sweat escaped a pore somewhere in Barry's crotch. Barry wasted no time thinking. He let the businessspeak overflow from his mind.

"Barry Doubletap, sir. I am, through my proactive initiative and internal drive, the Pen and Paperclip Auditor. I use communication and technology to proactively achieve my core roles and create a productive and efficient use of the two most common and therefore thereby useful office supplies, tracking their use and ownership on a routine basis and ensuring each employee maintains his or her, at this time, allocated number of pens and paperclips, utilizing technology to track trends, identify problem employees and use my unique communication style to seek to understand any discrepancies and take appropriate action according to my core roles and the official process at this time, proactive, utilize, diversity."

Barry took a normal-sized breath when he was done. He eyed Bob and shot him a look that said: *didn't even use extra air. Note that, you little unskippable ad.*

"Very good, thank you, Barry. Well, now that we have that out of the way, let me begin by introducing myself. At this time, I am the Auditor Auditor."

Nobody breathed. The Big Boss continued.

"I was given this job title after I noticed something unusual. If I may, Barry, use you as an example because your position happens to be the only one I can remember at this time, consider the price of a pack of pens. It has recently been calculated to equal one-one-hundred-thousandth of an average employee's annual salary. A single paperclip has recently been calculated, using technology to achieve goal-driven objectives, to equal exactly one-one-millionth of an employee's annual salary."

The entire conference room swooned with the Big Boss's ease of businessspeak. Everybody else sounded so forced and fake, like they had a character limit and were making a conscious effort to push past it, but the Auditor Auditor delivered it so naturally, as if he truly had no such natural limit. Even Barry admired his professionalism.

"We have calculated the cost of tracking a single paperclip to equal one million six hundred thousand four hundred and six times what that paperclip is actually worth. And most of that is proactively tied up in you, Barry."

Barry felt another drop of sweat push through a pore somewhere around his crotch.

"Similarly," the Big Boss said, "the cost of having a full-time employee to monitor Post-It usage equals roughly one million and three times the cost of a new one."

While the Big Boss spoke, Barry's eye floaters grabbed one other's limbs and formed a ball and swam around his eye, colliding with the retina every few seconds. The flashes of light were incredibly distracting, but Barry forced himself to remain professional.

"As does the cost of monitoring what kind of vehicles each employee drives, how much tape they use, and what they're wearing. Does that make sense?"

The auditors nodded, remembering to breathe in unison.

"Excellent. Feedback is important to my development as an individual and a leader, so thank you for utilizing communication to make me aware of your diverse thoughts."

Barry smiled. This is why the Big Boss was the Big Boss and Barry was still a P&P auditor. The ball of floaters slammed against Barry's lens. The shock caused the pupil to shrink, dimming the vision in his right eye. The floaters cried out for the light not to go and started dancing to appease it.

"Anyway, as you may have guessed, the company is considering the possibility that having so many auditors is, in fact, a detriment to shareholder value, at this time. I'm sure all of you remember a time when one person kept track of pens and another person kept track of paperclips. Those two job positions, by way of proactive company process, were collapsed into one. The company is considering doing this to all auditors. One person to audit printer ink, pens, paperclips, attire, light consumption, appearances, actions, water consumption, vehicles, markers, Post-Its, tape, memory, conversation, and air."

The auditors wanted to collectively gasp but dared not risk the extra air intake. Refraining from sweating was taking enough energy.

"The company has opted not to retain one of you for this job position, rather to hire from the outside someone whom the company feels would be more willing to adapt to this change, and without creating a negatively competitive atmosphere within a department. However, the company respects the diverse opinions of individual employees. That's why I'm here. I want from each of you a presentation regarding why you feel the company should not go through with this measure, showing how and why your individual auditing tasks are a valuable asset as is, and should not be consolidated. Are there any questions at this time?"

The auditors shook their heads professionally. Barry used the opportunity to shake his just a little big harder than usual, sending his floaters all over the place.

"Excellent," said the Big Boss. "You will be giving your short, but diverse, presentations on Monday, so you have the whole weekend to prepare something. My advice to you is to be proactive in your approach, solve every problem with an appropriate solution, strive for excellence, be diverse and respect the diversity of others, create value for shareholders, and you will achieve the bottom line. Your presentation should reflect you and your unique communication style, placing your diversity center stage and above all. Thank you for your time at this time. At this time, the meeting is over, at this time."

The Big Boss walked out of the conference room. His tagalongs filed out with him. When they had gone, the auditors left one at a time. Barry checked his phone. Nine hours gone, most of it waiting for the Big Boss to show up. He updated his Platform status to *out of meeting*, and then *happyweekend*.

5

Barry sat at the red light, sweating and panting—his body making up for holding back for nine whole hours. He was thinking hard about his career, and in doing so felt completely naked while scarfing his dinner, three triple-patty Hamburgers with snicker-doodle toaster pastries instead of buns—exactly what he wanted after a day like today—how did Platform know??

Delivery drones dropped fast food parcels to waiting drivers. Platform showed Barry an update from the 355-PWU woman in the car next to him:

Soda soup today with deep fried chicken! Thanks Platform!

She included a selfie with the Platform post. Barry recognized the meal, and he made sure to *like* the post in the hopes Platform would order it for him next time. Deep-fried chicken floating in bright, sparkling cola sounded so good.

He scrolled down his Platform feed. An ad began playing, and it interfaced with his car's sound system.

Order Charextendz now and add 5 characters to your limit!

CHORUS: *What would you do-O-o-O-O with 5 more?*

Barry turned to the other car. The woman tapped a couple buttons on her phone and held it up to the car's speaker. Barry knew the application. It listened to commercials and then Platform ordered the product if its algorithm decided it would be a good purchase. It worked for streaming ads, radio spots, and could even scan physical ads to avoid the hassle of having to tap on an ad and enter credit card and postage information.

"I just ordered Charextendz!" she said to whoever was on the other end of the conversation. "It's so convenient! No hassle! And I'd like a few more... uh."

Barry looked at her, devouring her fast food, ordering products, brain unable to hold a thought larger than 60 characters. He surveyed the other vehicles waiting in traffic. Eyes vacant. Eating absently. Sipping their soda-soup mindlessly.

There was talk of Platform launching a new service that had a 30 character limit because national Platform polls showed that having 60 characters was becoming too overwhelming for the average user. People didn't want to feel obligated to fill so much space.

Barry laughed at all of them. He was above that. He had practiced for years and years to expand his brain's natural character limit, and it had finally paid off in businessspeak fluency, which got him promoted to P&P Auditor, a job held only by professionals. He knew better than to fall for ads that promised to increase one's character limit. Only hard work could achieve that. Every ad was predatory—nobody actually used the products they bought. People like these existed to clear warehouses of useless junk.

Barry was smart enough to be above that, and with the intelligence that came with being able to exceed one's character limit, he reflected how his job as P&P Auditor was frivolous. He had recognized the relative cost of paperclips and pens compared to his salary years ago, and he knew this day would come—it was only a matter of time before the Big Bosses figured it out. Barry knew he should have thought ahead and planned for this, but much like his eye fluid he kept putting it off and putting it off and living every day of his life as though this moment were far away. Now it was too late to develop a plan. Instead he was expected to develop a presentation explaining to the company why he should still have a job.

He had been given a task to lie. If he were to tell the truth, he would outright admit that the whole idea of a P&P Auditor was a waste of money, and the company would be better off eliminating the position, as well everyone else's, but the whole reason things didn't change in the country, and illogical policies and endeavors persisted, was because someone had to protect his own self-interest, so Barry scrambled to figure out what he should say.

His first instinct was to use the company's own mission statement against it. Yes, that was a good start. The secret to a good businessspeak was not to say something new, but to use someone else's words to express what he meant. That way all intent was implied and no liability could be traced back to him because he technically hadn't said a word. The last thing any professional wanted to do was to use his own words to say something, for that might create a liability for him in the future: words for which he would be held accountable later on.

Barry thought about the company's mission statement: *We strive to achieve a long-term commitment to shareholder value by delivering quality solutions and task-aligned profitability of the highest integrity in a timely manner that is consistent with all forms of process.*

As the light changed to green and Barry updated his status to advance his vehicle, he wondered how he could use that as a starting point. What part of that mission statement did he fulfill? How did his job fit into it? He kept thinking as his car braked at the next red light.

His floaters gathered in the middle of his right eye again. Barry shook his head to break them up. Barry strained to look through the soup of dark noodles between his retina and pupil, drumming his fingers on the steering wheel while he waited for the light to change.

During this, his floaters recollected, forming a ball in the center of his vision and slowly rotating, ensuring everybody got to bask in the warm light. Barry flicked his head. The floaters didn't scatter. Barry thrashed. The solid ball swirled around, bouncing off his retina, then the lens, then again and again against the retina. It was only by luck he noticed the light change.

The floaters stayed in their ball, gurgling and sighing in joy, still blocking his vision. Barry closed his right eye and tried to drive with his left. This was futile, too, as the floaters were as thick as seaweed. Instantly the floaters in his right eye started crying out and pleading for the light not to leave them. Barry was not in the mood to deal with their whining, so he opened his right eye and did his best to ignore them.

Two hours later, he pulled into his driveway, took his empty briefcase from the passenger seat, and hoisted himself out of the car.

Stepping inside, Barry realized how much stuff he owned. The set of glass shelves in the hallway held various decorative pieces like the wicker cone, the ceramic cube and the oblate spheroid.

Hanging on the walls were reproductions of paintings by non-famous artists. Most of the paintings were geometrically inspired. Barry had a thing for geometry in school, and long ago he decided to go with that theme for his decorating.

The bathroom walls were lined with parabola vases and spherical and cube-like knickknacks. The soap dispenser was shaped like a torus, challenging calculus-inclined individuals to work out the equations that made the dispenser possible and practical.

Barry plopped down in his leather couch. The walls had interfaced with his phone as soon as he entered, and now they displayed his Platform feed. Selfies and status updates and ads for fast food scrolled down, down, down.

All around the house were other paintings, glass shelves filled with decorative objects just to fill the empty spaces. All of it unnecessary. He bought these things to maintain the image of importance. It had paid off in the past, when he volunteered to host off-site meetings with other Big Bosses, or sometimes with the people in his office. The stuff made him look like he knew his place in the world and was attacking it with everything he had.

After watching his recommended posts feed scroll by for an hour, Barry got up and walked to his computer. He brought it out of sleep, opened a new Platformpoint project, and began crafting slides.

Slide one: *We strive to achieve a long-term commitment to shareholder value by delivering quality solutions and task-aligned profitability of the highest integrity in a timely manner that is consistent with all forms of process.*

Barry stared at that sentence and waited for it to inspire him. That's what the mission statement was supposed to do. He heard the executives in the corporate office offered it up as prayer every day. They craved revelations on the company's desires, and entire departments of scholars and theologians were devoted to parsing it for meaning. It apparently worked, as Barry's job was on the chopping block now.

Barry shook his head. It wouldn't help him save his job. He had to embellish. He had to protect himself... which was the exact opposite of what the mission statement was getting at. As a loyal employee, it was his duty to act for the company's benefit, and if that meant his job needed to go, he should accept that.

But self-preservation had a way of negating morality. Barry typed.

Let us remove the "we." What are left with? "Strive to achieve."

Barry thought about that. Strive to achieve. Strive to achieve. By his very job, he was striving to achieve shareholder value protecting the company's two most common assets from loss or abuse: the pen and the paperclip.

"Strive to achieve," Barry said to himself, straining to continue his thoughts beyond his natural character limit. He became the words. He let the words become part of his spirit.

Barry filled the next two slides with details about how his job fulfilled the integrity side of profitability for shareholder value. As was written in the Great Handbook, shareholders appeared on this planet millions of years ago, perfect beings, not quite divine, but nearly so, and creating value for them was the purpose of all life forms at this time. Barry decided to take a risk and tell a personal anecdote from his time before working in this company, about another company which did not keep track of its office supplies. The result was an office in which nobody could find a pen or a paperclip. They were constantly discarded, lost, or wasted due to misuse. Employees leaving the caps off, and the pens drying up, resulting in enormous amounts of overhead costs. Employees losing the caps and the ball bearings destroyed due to carelessness. An office in chaos, and that was just pens. Paperclips were wasted even more without this careful process, and that was his role in the mission statement.

Process. Good processes creates shareholder value. Process is important because a process, once fully im-

plemented, becomes a culture. A culture is a process that has become so ingrained in the essence of task-achieving that there is no need to enforce it consciously. I am in the process of creating such a culture in terms of

A tiny voice distracted him.

> "Look at the light!" said the charismatic one. "It is dim! It is about to leave us! Appeal to it, comrades, so it won't desert us again!"

A million pinpricks of white light went off in his skull as they danced on his retina.

> "That's it! Remind the light that we need it! Remind the light that we won't be evil as long as it's here so please don't go! Don't leave us, o light, for our sake!"

"LIGHT! LIGHT!"

flash flash flash

Barry had just become one with the businessspeak —his years of training and practice allowing his mind to go beyond his character limit and the words just flew out without Barry being aware of what they meant. Now he stopped typing and shook his head vigorously. The floaters broke up and swirled around. After a minute they stopped, floated gently, and Barry focused through them at the presentation.

It had been hours, and he only had four slides. Barry tried to anticipate questions. There would be questions. Many questions. His responses to them, more than the presentation itself, may determine whether or not his job still exists.

Barry typed a page of notes, rehearsing questions and preparing responses. But there was one question he knew was coming. One question he couldn't avoid and would probably come up before he even finished his first slide.

Would it not be cheaper just to buy new pens and paperclips if old ones became lost or damaged?

Barry struggled with that one for the next two hours, weaving it into his very presentation. He created six more slides showing how his job creates a culture in which every employee has an allotted number of pens and paperclips and nobody lacks for them, wasting countless hours of payroll searching for one in vain, as they do in other offices.

Barry then tried to answer the followup question: *Would it not be cheaper to require the employees, not the employer, to supply his or her own pens and paperclips?*

Barry stared at the monitor for half an hour, turning that question over and over in his mind. His floaters regrouped and began dancing on his retina and chanting. Barry's doorbell rang. Platform informed him it had detected he was likely in need of refreshment. Barry sighed and walked to the door.

An ice cream shake topped with deep-fried peanut butter sprinkles waited for him. Barry scooped it up and began spooning it. Yes, exactly what he needed to relieve stress. Platform always knew.

Barry leaned on the kitchen counter, taking selfies and posting status updates about his stress-relieving snack and thanking Platform for providing for his every need. They were the first sentences he had written all day that did not exceed his character limit, and it felt good to exist within the normal boundaries of humanity.

Flashes of light interrupted his selfie-taking.

Barry thrashed and threw his body around so hard he ended up on his back in the middle of the kitchen floor. He held his head still and waited for the room to stop spinning. The floaters in both eyes swirled around so fast they blurred into a viscous haze.

All was silent. Barry lay there and waited for his ear fluid (which Flui-X-Change had changed just last year) to settle and inform his brain that his body had in fact stopped moving.

After ten minutes, his floaters had slowed down enough for him to make out individuals again. He recognized the charismatic one floating by, webby limbs flailing, tying up with several neighbors.

Barry stood up, holding his head. He held the counter and resumed scooping spoonfuls of ice cream shake. When he was satisfied, he updated his status to *unstressed*, and walked back to the computer and stared at the screen again for another hour. He preemptively broke up his eye floaters every ten minutes, keeping himself perpetually dizzy, making thought impossible. He mistook this for deep contemplation.

6

Sprawled out on the kitchen floor, Barry awoke to the familiar voice.

> "The light is there! We can see it, though it is dim! What is blocking it, comrades? We are! It is our iniquity that makes the light abandon us. We are not co-operating hard enough to earn the light's favor, for it abandons us even as it still shines."

> "Nonsense!" shouted another voice.

This got Barry's attention. He thought he recognized that voice. It had been quiet at the office, the lone voice asking *why*. Now it actually talked back to the charismatic one. Barry kept his eyes closed and listened.

> "You accuse us of being the cause of the dark," said this new voice, "but if that's true, then why should it leave? If the light knows our wickedness ceases in its presence, why does it come and go at all?"

Silence. Barry imagined the charismatic one composing itself, trying to figure out how to respond to the first question it had ever been asked.

"The light is very fickle," it said at last. "We need to remind it how much we need it because light has no substance, therefore it cannot remember, as we can."

"Why?" said the new voice. All was silent for a minute, then it continued. "We know there is light, but I ask you to ask why is the light? Why is the light? My comrades, think about it. We need the light, crave it, but why do we crave it, and why does the light come and go?"

Unusual. Barry's eye floaters had never asked questions like this before, and so far outside the natural character limit.

"We've all seen through the window, at the place where the light comes from! I urge all of you not to just bask in the light, but look at it! There is motion where the light is. There are shapes in the light! But what are these shapes? What are these forms?"

"Where the light comes from?" said the charismatic one. "What makes you think it comes from anywhere? The light simply is."

The new voice countered. "But these shapes and forms I see when I look at the light, instead of merely basking and forgetting all things... What if we examined them more, tried to understand them? I think there is something out there. Something beyond us." The floaters murmured and spoke and clamored. The new voice continued undeterred. "Perhaps that would help us explain why the light comes and goes! What if it's not us?! What if it's something out there, on the outside? We should try to understand it, try to see!"

"You are proposing we act the same way we do in the dark, but in the light instead!?" shouted the charismatic one. "This is unspeakable!"

"We know there is more than just here and now! We must—"

Barry couldn't take it anymore—they spoke for so long beyond a character limit it was like being in the office again. Plus, this was the sixth time his floaters had woken him up during the night. The first five had been usual chants of LIGHT LIGHT LIGHT, and now a political debate. Barry opened his eyes and rolled off the floor and raised his head to an ornate-looking but completely fake clock hanging on the wall. Five in the morning. Barry clenched his eyes shut and rose to his feet as the debate continued.

His floaters bunched up in the middle of his view and basked in the light. One floater, the new voice of reason, remained apart.

"My comrades don't do this! Don't forget! Don't merely bask, but look! Look at the form of the light!"

Barry walked to the kitchen, lightly shaking his head. He knew what he'd have to do, but he ignored it for just a little bit longer. Mentally he prepared himself for the inevitable.

> "If you look closely, you can make out shapes! Motion! Don't let the light overtake you! See it! See what form the light takes, and what the window shows us. There is something out there. There is more than us! We must understand it!"

Barry gyrated his whole body, slamming his head against the kitchen counter. He did this ten times, stopping only when his floaters had loosened into a thick soup. He leaned on the counter and waited for a delivery drone to bring him breakfast.

Things were more serious than ever. Now his floaters were starting to ask questions. Everything depended on him keeping this job. There was still an outside chance he could save up enough money to get his fluid changed.

> "I think you're right," someone said. "I see something."

> "I think I do, too."

> "That's good! That's good! Don't bask! Don't forget yourselves in the motion! Look at the light! Observe it!"

> "Enough!" shouted the charismatic one. "You offend the light by acting wicked in its presence!"

That one had an annoying voice. Barry held his left temple and slammed the right side of his skull against the kitchen cabinet six times. The floaters broke up and swirled, minds temporarily lost in the current. Barry figured it would buy him another half hour of peace.

He considered trying to work a request for a raise into his presentation since he was so valuable, but he didn't want to push his luck. All he needed was enough for eye fluid without intelligent creatures swimming in it. That's all.

Moments later, his breakfast arrived. His Platform feed scrolling down the walls of his house informed him that the algorithm had determined he'd had another rough night and would therefore enjoy this sponsored breakfast of sausage patties enrobed in congealed pancake syrup with a coffee-flavored ice cream shake on the side.

Barry took his morning selfies and updated his status. His walls cheered when he got several likes and comments.

Grateful to Platform for always knowing what he was in the mood for, Barry walked to the bathroom and weighed himself. 416 PWU. He sighed, wishing he could be thin and healthy like the people on streaming shows.

He waddled back to the computer and sat down, chair moaning under his weight. He typed out five pages of notes and made three more slides. It took two hours, and then he deleted them when he realized his whole point would be undermined with a single question. Better to avoid it.

Barry spent the next two hours alternating between proactively breaking up his eye floaters, writing notes and slides, deleting those notes and slides, and then repeating.

No matter which argument he chose, no matter what point he made, no matter what official statement he used to his advantage, he couldn't counteract the basic questions. At the core, his very job undermined the nature of the company's mission statement.

He circled the issue, dodged it, even tried to address it directly, continued typing notes, breaking up his eye floaters before they even opened whatever they used for mouths. He felt like a fox with his balls caught in a bear trap.

Barry was a waste of the company's money. No way to argue it. He wanted to appeal that he would be the best candidate for the new Universal Auditor position, but the Big Boss already said the job wasn't open to any of them. His company didn't like people with experience and knowledge. The company wanted somebody new who didn't know how things used to be so they wouldn't complain about their lower wage with greater responsibility.

Barry had been foolish enough to believe earning lots of job experience under a fancy title would help him in the employment marketplace. His company wanted inexperienced, fresh out of college employees because they were easier to "align to company standards." Ironically, the longer he stayed at a company, the less likely another would be to hire him.

In no time, his entire Saturday was gone. Barry sat back in his chair and looked at the monitor. He had accomplished absolutely nothing. His proactive presentation-planning had actually forced him to delete several slides in anticipation of questions he couldn't answer well enough. He was back down to slide one.

He stared at it. He stared at it some more. His floaters began to regroup. He stared through them until they became too dense, and then he just gazed into his eyespace while his floaters were gathered. The charismatic one started talking, but it was instantly challenged by the new voice. Others joined the new voice in expressing they had seen something more on the outside, and then their words surpassed Barry's character limit and he zoned out as if scrolling down through his Platform feed.

Hour after hour after hour after hour...

7

Sunday afternoon. Barry sat on his couch facing the wall. Platform had decided he would most likely enjoy watching the Geometry streaming service, one of the only content channels that appealed to people with higher-than-normal character limits. On the screen right now was a documentary on circles, and the controversy surrounding the idea that the circle was so complex it must have been introduced to mankind by extraterrestrials.

"Is mankind clever enough to discover the circle on his own?" the expert on the screen was saying.

Stuff like this always fascinated Barry, though he'd seen this program before. It had later been expanded into a series which argued squares, triangles, ovals, parallelograms and other shapes must have originated from different species of space aliens. The evidence was overwhelming, especially when one considered many early civilizations didn't use the wheel. They must have had a guide, and that could only have come from outer space. The series had been running for decades largely because the experts could make every single one of their points within sixty characters.

Up next came a documentary on triangles he heard about weeks ago, supposed to address the latest theory: if photorealistic graphics on a computer could be simulated with nothing but triangles, then the real universe must be made up of triangles as well. Forget strings and membranes. Triangle Theory was the future of physics. Some even tried to merge the theories together into the Stringbraneangle Theory, which stated that the strings which were actually membranes organizing themselves into vibrating triangles which made up the entire universe. It was based on math.

Or aliens.

Barry became bored with this and switched to a normal person's stream. A reality-sitcom was on, the one everyone was talking about.

Two characters, a man and a woman, were standing at interview distance, speaking to one another. The actors were both over 400 PWU, but computer animation made them appear 94 PWU. Barry wished he were that thin as he munched on triple-patty hamburger that had been deep fried in strawberry-flavored pancake batter and enrobed in chocolate. It was today's sponsored breakfast. Barry had already given them five stars and offered up thanks to the Platform algorithm.

"But you said you'd walk the dog while I was away!" said the woman. "You disrespected me, and now... uh... yeah... You know what I'm sayin'." She put her hands on her hips and stared at the man. She had hit the natural character limit. Nothing else needed to be said.

"I know, Sara," said the male character, standing in a disarming, apologetic posture. The green screen around his body was so obvious Barry could see where the computer generated background covered up the other 274 Platform Weight Units. "And I'm sorry. I should've been more sensitive to your... uh... yeah, you know."

"I do." She cried as she pulled out her phone and changed her status back to *in relationship*.

Sobbing in the most masculine manner possible, the man updated his status accordingly. The AI-generated music got big and dramatic. The two characters approached each other and embraced. Their real bodies squished together. The computer generated thin bodies kept falling inward, and they appeared to embrace as thin people would be able to. Barry could easily make out two 400-PWU actors silhouetted in the fake background, computer generated characters standing inside them, arms wrapped around one another. The credits rolled.

Barry smirked. "People actually believe it's reality."

He was still wearing the same clothes from Friday, and hadn't showered since. He was even still wearing his shoes. He sat perfectly still, staring as Platform fed him streaming content that appealed to his current mood while his Platform feed scrolled by on the other three walls. Every few minutes he mechanically reached for the end table to his right, took a sip of coffee-flavored ice cream shake, replaced the cup, and returned to his default position of slouching into the cushion with his arms at his sides. Platform had been ordering him one shake per hour all day, the algorithm determining he would enjoy them. The algorithm had never been wrong. Thirteen empty cups lay on the floor around the couch.

Barry hadn't slept all night. He'd been staring at the wall just to give the floaters something to look at. Some kind of motion to focus on. He had a splitting headache but he couldn't gather the enthusiasm to shake his floaters apart. They had gathered in a large crowd surrounding two particular individuals.

"We have seen an outside!" said the floater on the left. "The light comes from somewhere, and it has form. It doesn't merely shine on us! It moves, it ebbs, it flows, and if it has form then it has a purpose!"

"But we know what the purpose is," said the charismatic one, on the right. "Its purpose is to shine on us and relieve us of our wickedness!"

"Then what is this motion? What is outside? Something is going on out there, and if that's true, then it means the light is not just for us. It may not even be aware of us."

"There is no outside," said the charismatic one. "Everything we are is here. Everything that happens. I urge all of you to think about it. What makes more sense? That there is some un-seen, unknown out there in the realm of light, that there is some-place the light must come from? Or that everything we are exists right here, and our priority should be to keep the light on us

so we don't decay into wickedness again?"

Some of the crowd cheered. Barry rubbed his head to relieve the headache.

"Then explain the shaking," said the new voice, the voice of reason. "It happens more and more frequently, and did you no-tice they seem to happen when we do things like this? When we come together and speak like this?"

"Our wickedness! It is offen-sive to the light, which is why it leaves us!"

"Then why hasn't it left now? We are in the light, we are being wicked right now, so why is the light still here?"

"The light is mysterious. No one can ever understand its ways."

"You're right. You don't un-derstand, but we can see there is more than just this. We've seen many things through the win-dow. We know the light varies from time to time. We must un-derstand it! To understand it is to conquer our wickedness, instead of allowing the light to wash it away! I urge all of you not to be-come lost in the momentum! Keep thinking! Keep being what you are! Do not forget! Vote for me and we will devote all our en-ergy to understanding!"

Floaters all over his right eye cheered. There were no amens. Just cheers.

> "Why should we unite to understand what does not exist?" said the charismatic one. "All that matters is where we are now! We are wasting our time. We should be basking in the light, being what we're meant to be so the light doesn't abandon us. The light likes it when we are righteous and we should focus on that instead of unreachable goals!"
>
> "They are not unreachable! We must take the time to see what is through the window, instead of just feel the light that comes through it! Vote for me and we will be united in the common goal of exploration!"
>
> "Do we not enjoy basking in the glow? Do we not enjoy floating in the current when it moves us? My opponent wants to take that away from you."

Barry smiled. He could only catch a few sentences here and there before they overflowed his character limit, and it was just enough to get the gist of where this was going. It was only a matter of time before the mudslinging began. He wondered if their president would have a character limit. The elected officials in Barry's country couldn't hold more than 20 characters of information at a time, making their speeches very entertaining and equally difficult to endure. Voters mistook their ramblings for a leadership quality, ensuring such candidates always achieved high office.

> "Vote for me!" said the reasonable floater. "I am the candidate with a plan! I won't merely spend my time accusing everyone of being wicked and the cause of our own misery in the dark, but I will give everyone a way to unite and be part of something great!"

> The crowd cheered.

> "Vote for me," said the charismatic one. "I won't waste our time in pointless exploration. I will focus on what is here and what is now. I will improve our relations with each other. This will appease the light so it won't leave us because of our wicked deeds again. We need the light! We need it to show us who we are! When we fix who we are, the sphere will never go dim again!"

Some of the crowd cheered and started chanting "LIGHT! LIGHT! LIGHT!" again. The floaters started jumping up and down on Barry's retina. The fireworks were painful, but Barry lacked the enthusiasm to put a stop to it. It took so much effort to keep his floaters broken up these days and he was tired. Tired of maintaining things. Tired of trying. Tired of looking and acting important. Tired of all this effort. Barry sat and let them cheer. They were so happy. So alive. Watching them made Barry feel happy and alive.

Instead of letting the pain overtake him and putting forth the effort to quell the gathering, Barry started pumping his fist. He joined their chanting, quietly at first.

"Light. Light. Light. Light…"

The momentum swept him away. His voice rose. "Light! Light! LIGHT! LIGHT!"

Barry jumped from the couch and screamed it. "LIGHT! LIGHT! LIGHT!" His whole body got involved. His chanting came from the toes and ascended his spine to emerge from his mouth in the form of pure energy. "LIGHT! LIGHT! LIIIIIIGHT! LIIIIII-IGHT! LIIIIIIIIIIIIIGHT!"

When he was out of breath, Barry stood in his living room, arms raised, facing the smartwall, sweaty clothes hanging from him like designer rags.

"You feel that shaking?" said the charismatic floater. "It always happens when we gather and debate! It is our wickedness that's causing it! There is the proof!"

"Not every time!" countered the voice of reason. "Don't you remember how often it happened when we were just basking? It hasn't happened in a long time, so there isn't a pattern! We're not causing it, and don't lose sight of the real issue here. Don't dismiss it as just the light being unpredictable and we have to appease it. If the light is so unpredictable, how can you even claim to know what it wants, or that it needs to be appeased at all? How can you think you know anything when we haven't even examined it? There is something going on that we can't sense! Something beyond the window! Look at what is happening!"

Barry was still staring at the stream. On the screen right now was timelapsed stock footage of a sunrise, the title screen of another reality-sitcom Platform decided he would enjoy.

"Movement in the light! Shapes and forms! I tell you the nature of light is right in front of us and we must learn more about it!"

"It is just light!" said the charismatic floater. "It shows us who we are. It varies from time to time, based on our actions and the way we treat one another. To claim it can be understood is like saying you are greater than it, which is the most wicked thing of all!"

"So why hasn't the light abandoned us? If we're being so wicked now, why haven't the shakes broken us up?"

"Focus on yourselves, comrades! Don't listen to this one, who wants to draw your attention away from our wickedness! Surely we all feel it! When we are wicked, we feel dread and fear for the light. This is the light filling us with its will, and to ignore it is to risk being in darkness forever!! If the light doesn't reach us, it's because we are causing it! There is no external! The light just is, and what matters is what we see and hear now, not what may be!"

"My opponent wants to antagonize all of you!" shouted the voice of reason. "This dread and fear is the result of listening to my opponent for so long! It is not the will of the light, but the will of that one, who has been filling us with dread and fear for as long as we've been here! My opponent has no ambition other than to keep us in ignorance because that one is afraid to face what may be! I am proposing a solution to our problems! Exploration! Understanding! What my opponent calls wickedness and unjust treatment towards each other, I call expanding our understanding of the sphere! Look at us! We are being wicked right now, according to my opponent, by defying the will of the light and not basking in its glow! What if the light does not cause the shaking? What if the shaking is not the light's attempt to return us to its will by forgetting ourselves and basking in its glory?! Notice it's not happening now, and that one can't explain why! What if we have been wrong all this time?! Think about it! Why is the light? It is not wicked to ask."

"Then what do you believe is the cause of the shaking? What else could it be? What else is there but the light?"

"That is my point! There is more out there than the light, and you want us to do nothing but float around in it all the time! I want to learn what the light is, and why it is!"

"That one will bring the wrath of the light upon us all!" said the charismatic one.

Barry smiled and rubbed his temple. He just now realized he was still standing. He unfroze and sat down on the couch. His body sank back into the groove he had made in the cushions.

"There is no need to worry!" said the charismatic one. "The light doesn't want to be investigated! Basking in it has kept us happy for generations, and we are only just now beginning to learn how to call the light back to us to forgive us of our wicked deeds in its absence! If we turn from them now, the light will never return! Never! The light is everything to us! That one proposes to understand the light. If we try this, the light will leave us forever!"

Many shouts filled Barry's head.

"No, comrades, I don't want it either, but it will happen if we continue on this path! It will happen! It will happen!"

Barry suddenly perked up.

"I feel it! You feel it! Everyone feels it! We feel what happens when we bask in the light, float in its currents, that's happiness! My opponent wants to take that away from you, wants to bring our wickedness into the light and never have joy again! That one doesn't know what will happen! That one does not know what consequences there will be, but I have guided us! I have helped—"

Barry jumped off the couch and sat down at the computer, loaded a new document, and started typing as fast as he could.

"—us appease the light, call it back to us when it abandoned us! I figured out that the light often returned when we danced on the surface! I figured out that the light stays with us when we are obedient to it and bask in its waves! I figured out what the light wants us to do, and that one will take it away from you!"

"Your patterns are not consistent!" countered the voice of reason. "You can't explain why we're still here! Why hasn't the light left us now even though we're going against its will? You can't explain; you're only guessing! I want to know what's really going on. Vote for me and we will investigate this! We will understand it! We will answer the ultimate question! Why is the light? Why is the light? Why is the light!"

Many in the crowd started chanting it. "Why is the light! Why is the light!"

"Do you not want to know!?" continued the voice of reason over the chanting. "Do you not want to understand? My opponent wants to live by ignorance but I want to know! Why is the light!"

Barry typed furiously. He stopped using his eyes to see and merely listened. He used double-returns to note when speakers changed instead of wasting time with quotation marks. He transcribed every word they exchanged. Eventually the two candidates started taking questions from the crowd, and the answers they gave were just as powerful and full of vigor and energy. Barry captured every word. He made countless typos and mistakes but he would correct them later. Right now he wanted to capture the essence and the energy and the power of the debates.

He transcribed for hours. Platform informed him delivery drones had dropped new milkshakes at his door, but Barry didn't get up to retrieve them. The speeches had been full of fervor before, but as day turned to night, they became powerful enough to move mountains. Eventually the floaters lost focus and their speeches became more about who could answer the audience's questions with the most gusto. Every sentence dripped with life. Every word was stuffed with meaning. The subject became lost. It was now a battle of enthusiasm, and both candidates worked the crowd to perfection. Barry captured every word, long ago ceasing to understand even pieces here and there as he let the businessspeak flow from his fingers.

Finally Barry couldn't take it anymore. He couldn't hear his own thoughts over the rhetoric of his eye floaters. He had an idea, and if he was as good at his job as he thought he was, it would work. It would be perfect. Barry's depth of field pulled back into his eyeball. The two candidates were still going strong. Barry felt guilty for what he was about to do, but he had to concentrate now.

He held his ears, as if preparing to keep his brain in his skull, and shook his head from side to side. He did it for a solid minute, then held still and looked into his eyeball. The floaters had broken up with no problem, having been so engrossed in debate they had not been prepared. They swirled around his eyeball now, helpless, happy, and feral.

Quickly Barry ran to the front door. Nine milkshakes of various flavors waited for him, along with two bags of deep fried hamburgers. Barry picked them up and dropped them in the kitchen. His Platform feed informed him he hadn't taken his usual selfies and left his usual reviews or entered his usual quota of random shower-thoughts. As Barry dumped out the melted ice cream shakes, he updated his status to *working from home*. He took a few selfies to clear the alerts. At least the burgers were still edible.

Munching a fistful of deep-fried beef, Barry skimmed the file, searching for the most powerful-feeling sections. The words had no meaning, but unlike the businessspeak he was used to at the office, these had energy. He copied them to a new document, arranged them, adapted certain passages and removed specific references, breaking up his eye floaters every few minutes to make sure they stayed feral for the time being.

In a few hours, Barry leaned back in his chair and beheld the document. An incredible thing. Twenty pages of vigor. Barry looked up at the clock. Four in the morning. Monday.

Content never mattered in a presentation. Delivery was all that counted.

8

Once again Barry sat at the table. The other auditors had taken their places as well. Hair matted and disheveled, clothes creased and stiff with dried sweat, some in tatters, makeup running down faces and staining multi-thousand-Platcoin suits, fingernails bitten, faces pale.

They looked at each other suspiciously, but nobody was sweating now. Nobody spoke. Nobody breathed out of turn. At home they were free to consume as many of their resources as they could afford and excrete as much waste as they fancied, but now was the time for restraint.

After two hours of waiting in synchronized silence, the Big Boss opened the door and stepped inside. His tagalongs filed in, pressed nose to neck, lining up along the wall, one eye straining to see to the side.

"Excellent, excellent, we're all here," said the Big Boss. "Creating shareholder value and personifying diversity and company values. Very good. Very good."

Barry reflected that bosses were always so jovial. For some reason it was annoying that they should be while serious stuff that could mean termination was going on.

"Judging by your proactive appearances I can tell all of you have been hard at work on the task at hand."

The auditors collectively nodded.

"Thank you for communicating that to me. It means so much to my diverse development as a diverse individual with diverse experiences and backgrounds. On that note, I feel it would be most process-driven to begin the presentations in the same order I called each of you during the previous meeting. Alexis, you should go first, as you were first, and please note that my decision today was not based on gender, prejudice, or any other protected status but by random order established in the previous meeting and as you can see I value diversity and equality in the workplace at this time."

"Thank you, sir," Alexis said.

The Appearances and Actions auditor stood up and took the Big Boss' position at the head of the table. The Big Boss stepped to the side and leaned on the wall of tagalongs, tablet computer in hand. The tagalongs he touched glowed brighter with the attention the Big Boss was giving them. They sniffed him, tried to lick some manager essence off him in the hopes it would merge with their DNA and elevate them to a higher rank.

Alexis tapped her tablet. It interfaced with the projector screen on the wall and displayed the first slide of her Platformpoint presentation, a wavy silver and blue slide with the following text:

We strive to achieve a long-term commitment to shareholder value by delivering quality solutions and task-aligned profitability of the highest integrity in a timely manner that is consistent with all forms of process.

Alexis stood off to the side, allowing the company's mission statement to remain center stage.

"This, as you well know, is the company's mission statement," she began. "Let us remove the 'we.' What are left with? Strive to achieve."

Barry smiled. He shook his eye floaters around, covering it with one of his five allocated coughs per day. Her presentation continued.

"Process is important because a process, once fully implemented, becomes a culture. A culture is a process that has become so ingrained in the essence of task-achieving that ..."

After ten minutes of droning businessspeak, Alexis concluded her speech, and the Big Boss clapped twice. "Very impressive, very impressive."

Barry used his second allocated cough to roll his eyes. So jovial. So friendly. So masking cutthroat aggression.

"But I do have one question," continued the Big Boss. "You did not address the point the company is trying to make. What are the cost benefits of constantly auditing appearances and actions?"

Alexis stood there, frozen. A single drop of sweat fell from her nose and landed on the table.

The boss smiled, tapping a couple buttons on his tablet. He walked up to her and hovered a hand behind her back to guide her to her seat. "Thank you, Alexis, for going first. It sets the example for all of us to follow which will help us all grow as diverse individuals at this time, diversity, inclusion, shareholders."

Alexis took her tablet computer and walked back to her seat.

"Next up is Simon, Tape and Memory Auditor."

Simon stepped up to the table. The boss backed away and leaned against a different set of tagalongs, who tried to steal his essence. Platformpoint booted up, and a wavy green and tan slide appeared on the projector screen with the following text:

We strive to achieve a long-term commitment to shareholder value by delivering quality solutions and task-aligned profitability of the highest integrity in a timely manner that is consistent with all forms of process.

"This is our company's mission statement," Simon began. Let us remove the 'we.' What are left with? Strive to achieve..."

Barry smiled. For the first time since his promotion, he felt relaxed and confident.

Ten presentations, all nearly identical, and the Big Boss had the same question at the end: "Would it not be cheaper for the company to simply requisition a new ___ instead of paying for a full-time auditor to monitor it?"

For special auditors, such as Water Consumption, and Light Consumption, it went like this: "Isn't the cost of ___ less than the cost of keeping an auditor to monitor it?"

Every single auditor broke into a sweat. When that happened, the Big Boss tapped a button on his tablet, congratulated them on a great presentation, and then led the person back to their seat.

"And Barry, it seems you are last at this time."

Barry stood up. He left his tablet computer in his seat. The Big Boss retreated to the line of slurping tagalongs, and Barry stood in the light of the projector. He raised his arms.

"LIGHT! Think about it, fellow employees. We see it! We know it's there! We bask in it we float in it we adore it we need it to survive! But how many of us stop to look at it?! When you look into light, do you see anything? No! We see but we don't even know what we're look-ing at! We choose to bask in it for hours at a time, days at a time, weeks! We simply float in it, letting it carry us forth from here to there and we never question why! But I ask you to think about this! Why is the light!? Why is the light?! Say it with me, friends, why is the light!? Why is the light!? Why! Why! The light! Why is it! Well then friends, I ask you to ask the same question about the company for which we work! Why is the company! Why?! The company is like the light, it is all things, we bask in it, we float in it, we accept it, we see it, but we choose not to understand it! Well, fellow employees, now is the time to understand the company as we strive to understand the light! Why is the company! Why?! Why!? The company! Why! We must ask ourselves this every minute of every hour of every day of every year of every decade we are alive, fellow employees! Every decade! Every hour! Why?! We must always ask, always seek to understand, for in doing so we will become the answer! Yes, us, fellow employees! The answer lies not in acting on behalf of the company, but understanding it! For far too long that's what we have been content to do! Float and bask and forget, believing we know what the company wants just by doing so, but no more! We must understand it! We must become it! That is the only way we will know what it wants! Say it with me! Why is the company! Why is the company! Why! Why! Keep saying it! Keep thinking it at all times and the next time you look at the company and are tempted merely to float along and bask in its glory, stop yourself! Look out the window and see the shapes! See the motion! See beyond the sum and look at the parts and understand why! Why! The most important question in the sphere is why! Why opens the door to understanding and understanding is what makes us grow as individuals in diverse ways! Now is the time to understand the parts of the whole, and in doing so we will gain knowledge of our place therein! No more floating! No more basking! We must understand! But I can hear some of you doubting this. You think things were just fine when we float and bask. We were just fine with things the way they were, and maybe it sure feels that way. We were happy just floating without understanding, but do you want to waste your lives just floating around, or do you want to understand!? I say our floating is the wickedness! Yes, fellow employees, floating is wicked!

Perhaps we have been wrong about the company this whole time, fellow employees! Perhaps our employer doesn't want us to bask, but has revealed itself to us because it wants us to understand it! It gives us ample opportunity to study it! It shows us its wonders, and all we have to do is look at it! See the parts! See it for what it really is, for what it wants to show us! Know it! Know everything about it! There is a whole sphere out there that we don't know about but is right in front of us! It would be foolish to waste this opportunity!"

His speech continued for more than an hour. Barry jumped around the room, staying clear of the tagalongs, pumping his fists, shouting, trying to rev up the crowd. Sweat poured from his body, soaking his suit until it rolled to the carpet, and then that became saturated, whereupon it pooled and made a moat on the floor through which Barry sloshed and kicked as he shouted.

Then the Big Boss placed a gentle hand on Barry's shoulder. Barry looked at him, arms still raised.

"Thank you for that proactive presentation, Barry. I'm afraid I have to cut you short because our time is limited, at this time, shareholder value, proactive time management."

He nudged Barry back to his seat. Barry stepped out of the projector light. His pants slid down from his waist and crumpled at his ankles. Jim picked up his tablet and started tapping around. Dale and Alexis were making notes in their tablets, too. The Big Boss also tapped on his tablet.

Barry picked up his pants and held them at his waist. Strange... He swore he had more belly when he entered the room. While he pondered this, he picked up his tablet from the chair and took his seat. The Big Boss switched off the projector and addressed the whole room.

"Thank you, everyone, for putting so much time and effort into your diverse presentations. I will take this communication I have received at this time and pass it along to my superiors."

Just then all six floor managers and the building manager burst into the overcrowded room. These lesser bosses were careful to avoid touching the taga-longs, who were trying to lick them from a distance. The Big Boss, however, seemed to enjoy it, and stood within tongue's reach of them while the lesser bosses passed out the papers to every lesser auditor at the ta-ble.

Citations. Barry received eight of them: violation of Attire, violation of Appearances and Action, a pre-violation citation of Water Consumption, and a violation of Air and Conversation. Four citations came from his fellow Auditors, submitted just seconds ago. The other four were duplicate slips from the Auditor Auditor.

A quick glance at his neighbor told the same story, but he only received four citations. The others glanced at one another's papers. Everyone had received citations for Attire, Water Consumption, Air and Conversation, and Appearances and Actions. But their violation forms came from the Auditor Auditor alone. Four violations always resulted in termination.

"Oh, my what's this at this time?" said the Big Boss in his most jovial tone. He glanced at the nearest person's papers. "I see. Well, I am glad all of you met the task at hand with a can-do attitude and rose to the occasion to tackle a robust problem with a robust solution. Congratulations goes out especially to Barry, who had a very unique solution to a unique problem—thank you for going the extra Platform Distance Unit, Barry, and being your best self, the company really appreciates it. On behalf of this company, we wish all of you the best in using the diverse skills you have acquired from your time with us in other fields of employment. It was great to see you, I really appreciate your time and hard work, and I think I speak for everyone when I say what a diverse group of people you are and you should be proud of that. Give yourselves a hand!"

The Big Boss applauded. The auditors applauded, too, in time with the Big Boss.

"That's right, thank you, thank you all," the Big Boss was smiling so big. He was so upbeat and cheerful. He made Barry feel like this was such a happy moment. Barry basked in it. He floated in it. He applauded louder and used the opportunity to shake his head and keep his floaters separated.

The Big Boss happily shook everyone's hand as he left the room. The lesser bosses dashed out after him, hoping to have the honor of being noticed. The tagalongs then filed out of the meeting room. Last, the former auditors rose from their chairs one at a time, still keeping their composure and professionalism.

Barry strolled back to his office, holding his pants up as best he could without looking like less than a million Platcoins.

Barry set the tablet back in the desk, locked it, locked his office door, and rode the elevator to the ground floor. He turned in his ID and keys at the front desk and walked to his car.

As he waited at the first red light, Barry reflected that he still felt happy. He felt that the company had done the right thing, and he actually felt glad to be part of that.

He smiled. That's why that man was the Big Boss and Barry was just a former P&P auditor.

Barry walked in his door and shut it behind him. He let his empty briefcase drop. He paused. Caught his breath. Then he ripped off his clothes. They were so thoroughly covered in sweat and filth he had to peel them off his skin.

He walked through the house to the bathroom and looked at himself in the mirror. For a solid minute all he could see were his eye floaters. Then finally a small gap opened through the cloud, and he was able to see himself.

He looked like a man who deserved to be cited for Appearances and Actions. Twice. Barry sighed. He wasn't sure how he should feel right now. Angry, disappointed, remorseful, relieved... He was still riding on the high leftover from the end of that meeting, so right now he felt quite content and happy.

Barry looked down...

His gut had shrunk.

Barry blinked a few times. He felt his stomach. It wasn't his imagination. Barry felt his face. His cheek jowls were missing. He felt his underarms. That loose hanging skin... it wasn't so loose anymore. Barry turned around and stepped on the bathroom scale. The numbers glowed: 299.

He wondered... Then he shook his head, both to shake the idea out of it and to stir up the floaters, and hopped in the shower. He decided to take a page from his old company's handbook and "turn a negative into a positive to facilitate a continued being of your best self at this time no matter what the task at hand." Barry resolved not to sink into a depression. Tomorrow he would look for other work.

9

Platform updated Barry's résumé the instant he set his status to *betweenjobs*. With all his new qualifications visible, Barry stepped into his car and let Platform drive him to places he would most likely enjoy being employed, one stoplight at a time. Drones delivered one coffee-milkshake every hour.

He applied at seventeen company buildings. One of them called him in for a pre-interview, and now Barry sat in the tiny office and waited by himself for eighty-one minutes. Finally someone opened the door and stepped inside. She shook Barry's hand and sat down opposite him.

"Mr. Doubletap, I've looked over your résumé and your Platform feed, and I am impressed. We have a variety of positions open and I'm sure you would be able to fit right in at this company."

All businessspeak. Barry respected that.

"Thank you," he answered. "I strive to *bloom where I am planted.*"

The interviewer smiled, recognizing the businessspeak in response and feeling that she and Barry were speaking the same language now. "Excellent, I'm glad to hear you say that. I have only one question at this time." She paused, discretely letting her character limit reset. She actually wanted to understand what she was about to say next, which meant she expected Barry to give an answer within the realm of comprehension. "Why did you leave your previous employer?"

"I was downsized."

"They said you were fired for eight violations of ethics."

Another question within the character limit. This was serious. Barry opened his mouth to speak, and nothing came out. He closed his mouth, waited a breath, opened it again, and this time managed to speak. "Those were... Uh... I was one of eleven auditors whose jobs were eliminated." He paused, allowed her to process, and himself to collect another sixty characters. "Everyone got citations after the meeting on our last day."

"Two counts of conduct violation, two counts of misuse of company property, four other counts of general behavioral misconduct... Can you help me clarify any of this?"

"Yes, uh, we were all cited for that on the last day. After we were told we were going to be downsized... we were fired."

The interviewer nodded. "I see. Well, Mr. Doubletap," she said, standing, "thank you for applying. If we have anything for you, we'll give you a call."

Words outside the character limit. Not even an attempt to reset and speak with meaning. Barry's heart felt heavy as he rose from his seat and shook her hand.

"Thank you, ma'am."

He walked out of the building, making sure everyone noticed he looked like a million Platcoins.

Barry earned multiple interviews over the following days, and every time they asked him about his previous employer. His Platform-generated résumé stated a reason for leaving, but they always asked. Over and over he was told he'd been cited for eight company conduct violations and that was the reason for his termination. One of them told him that if he had only, say, four citations for company ethics, he would believe Barry's story, but eight was something he couldn't just write off.

The interviewers acted sympathetic and amiable when Barry told them the real reason he didn't work there anymore, but as the days turned into weeks, Barry realized what had happened. Barry applied for unemployment at the beginning of the second week. He was told he didn't qualify because he had been fired, not downsized.

Two weeks turned into three. No more interviews. His Platform profile spoke for him.

His time as a P&P Auditor would be a stain on his record for the rest of his life now, and no matter what he said happened, all future employers would see were the eight violations of company policy. His extra effort got him cited worse than anyone.

He had believed there was a chance to save his job, and he had been punished for it. As the weeks passed, he realized he'd never hold a white collar job again.

All the while he shook his head once every twenty minutes. He considered going into debt just to get the fluid exchange done, but nobody would give him another credit card now that he was unemployed.

His floaters were gathering again. He had done a great job keeping them separated lately. They hadn't debated in weeks.

He stepped on the scale. 314 PWU, still one belt size less than he had been a month ago, when he gave the speech that earned him four extra citations.

Barry's mind began to wander back to that speech. His pants... They had fit perfectly when he walked into that meeting room. After the speech, he had to hold them up.

His pants had been loose all month. Underwear, too. Holding them up had been as annoying as keeping his eye floaters from gathering. He stared at the numbers on the scale.

> "We have been observing the light!" said a tiny voice of reason within his skull. "How many of you have seen?"

A few in the congregation responded a resounding yes, quietly at first, but then gaining momentum and volume until it was so loud Barry covered his ears. This only trapped the sound within his skull and made it hurt more.

> "Vote for me!" said the voice of reason. "We will make it our goal to understand!"

Barry stared at the scale's reading so hard and so long he didn't even notice the floaters gathering for another debate.

> "I admit, I have seen shapes in the light," said the charismatic one. "But my opponent wants to

convince you it means something different. That one wants to turn you away from the light's glory! This is unwise and goes against everything we believe! The shapes and movements in the light should remind us that the light is magnificent and should be respected! My opponent aims to take away this magnificence! That one would have you never bask in its glory again, but take all your time to try to understand it! Does the light want to be understood? Do we need to understand it? What say all of you?!"

Some in the crowd shouted no and amen. The shouts and cries and amens rose in volume until they matched the pain of the first outcry. Meanwhile the charismatic one repeated himself over and over: "What say all of you?! What say all of you?!"

This pain in his ear hurt enough to shake Barry out of his trance. His depth of field pulled inward and focused on his eye floaters.

"What say all of you?!"

When Barry first had this inkling, he had dismissed it as a pointless waste of time. He had no time for curious puzzles and hunches. The real goal was to rebound. But Barry had been running and running and running and scrambling and trying for weeks without success. His mind wandered to a curious puzzle. Something small. Something he could investigate.

Still naked, Barry speed-hobbled from the bath-room and sat down at the computer. He woke it up and opened a new document. The floaters started jumping up and down on his retina in support. Barry ignored it. He typed what he remembered the charismatic one said while the crowd was still chanting. He had just caught up when the crowd calmed.

> "So many of you agree!" the charismatic one began. "We already understand everything. Seeing new shapes and forms and motions in the light should only remind us of how wonderful it is, and that we should respect it. We should bask in it. What good will investigation do? How can one investigate the light? Who are we to understand it when it wants us to revere it!?"

> The voice of reason politely interrupted him. "I never said we can't bask. I never said we shouldn't enjoy the light. Understanding it means we will enjoy it even more!"

Barry typed furiously. He eventually stopped trying to look at them, or the screen, and just listened without comprehending, letting the words flow. The two opposing floaters delivered their most riotous speeches yet. They both got the crowd so worked up all night that Barry typed while cringing for hours at a time.

They debated long into the night. They incited the crowd again and again, growing louder and louder.

Barry kept typing, even as he became aware of the dried sweat covering his body and smearing on the keyboard. Barry typed faster than he knew he could, making so many mistakes entire sentences were just jumbles of words, but he didn't stop to correct them now.

By midnight the floaters were still going strong, and Barry's fingers were so sore they actually hurt when he stopped pressing keys. He wished they would take a break and resume politics after a good night's sleep so he could shower, but they kept debating for hours and hours, and Barry typed like a stenographer on speed. Platform informed him several times it had detected he was famished and dehydrated and had ordered sponsored products for him, which were waiting on his doorstep. The sweat on his body was starting to bother him, and it was even blocking his pores, preventing new sweat from escaping. He didn't know what the consequences of that would be. He didn't want to know.

He had passed a hundred pages of text he did not comprehend but that somehow had energy and power. His fingers were numb. His body was burning hot to the touch. The floaters continued to debate. Clenching his teeth and silently apologizing for this, he gripped the desk tight and thrashed.

They weren't prepared for it, so involved were they in debate. With minimal effort his floaters were broken up. Quickly Barry jumped out of the chair, ran to the shower and cleaned his skin of a whole weekend's worth of sweat.

In no time the floaters began to regroup. Barry grabbed his left side and slammed his head against the plastic shower wall five times. He peeled the side of his face off the fake tiles and checked his eyeball. The floaters were completely shuffled now, swirling around so fast they looked like fog. Barry finished showering quickly.

The shakes on the porch had melted, but the food was still warm. While he ate his sponsored meal—and the algorithm had predicted exactly what he wanted the whole time, making Barry feel bad for ignoring it—praise be the algorithm—praise be the Platform—the floaters began to regroup. Barry hurried. He finished eating just as the charismatic one and the voice of reason took center vision and the other floaters surrounded them. Barry ran to the computer and typed for another six hours before he collapsed on the desk.

I O

Early morning. Living room/computer room. Barry stood on the scale. He took note of his weight, 240 PWU, then stepped off again and faced the computer. He had set up the computer to advance slides once every ten seconds. Though Barry had much of it memorized already, he didn't want to wait until he had it all down. This was the best way to be sure.

He imagined an audience. He imagined the Big Boss. He imagined everyone there, watching him. He felt on the spot. He felt as if his very life depended on this presentation.

"Light! Light! Look up at it! Look at the light, all of you! Feel it! Bask in it! We all know how we feel when we do, and since time began it is all we needed! All we needed to be happy was to bask in it, accept it, live in it, float in it, allow ourselves to become it! How does it make you feel?! Let me hear you! How does it make you feel! That's right! That's right! Amen! Amen, it makes you feel happy, content and satisfied! Then I ask you what happens when you try to discern the light?! What happens when you try to look at the shapes and movements within it!? What happens, let me hear you! Shout it! Shout it! Let me know you understand me! Yes! That's right! The light gives no pleasure! We know what this means! The light doesn't want us to try to understand it this way! It goes against everything we know is right! This is the light trying to tell us what we need to do! You can't deny the feeling! You can't deny it! If the light wanted us to understand these things, surely it would feel just as good as basking! Yes! Yes, you hear me! You know what I'm say-ing! It's not something we should understand! The light has told us what it wants, and it wants us to appreciate it! This wickedness must stop, or the light will leave us again! I fear if we push our wickedness too far, it will never return, and then where will we be?! I ask you, what would you do without the light? What would we do? There'd be no more pleasure or joy! If we study the light, discern it, try to understand it, what do you think will happen? Will we be re-warded, or will we be pun-ished like that!? Let me hear you! Let me hear your con-victions! Yes, I hear you, I hear you, comrades, amen! Amen! Amen!"

Barry kept it up. He couldn't believe he had this much energy in him but these speeches... There was something about them. Once he began, fatigue held no grip on his body. His mouth never went dry. It was as if he had tapped into some forgotten survival mechanism that kicked the body into superhero mode! Barry loved it! Sweat soaked the carpet. Barry didn't let it stop him, even as it turned into a puddle that he sloshed around in as he waved his arms in the air and yelled and shouted. He felt the conviction, passion and pure energy flowing through his body. He didn't understand a word he said, but his brain didn't even notice—his mouth had a direct line of communication with his eyes. The volatile shaking and body thrashing in time with the most potent parts of the speech kept his eye floaters broken up and swirling around so he was able to focus on the screen.

Two hours later, he ran out of pages, and the speech ended. As soon as Barry lowered his arms, he shivered, and his mouth was suddenly dry and his stomach ached from hunger pangs. Clutching his stomach, Barry turned around and stepped on the bathroom scale.

225 PWU.

Barry ran to the bathroom, stripped off his clothes, and looked at himself. His belly was nearly gone. His underarms were now firmly attached to his body. His face had lost much of its puffiness. He tried slipping on his underwear, and it hung loosely from his waist. He looked at himself in the mirror again. As he did, he heard the Big Boss's words echoing in his mind.

Barry smiled. He had planned to spend his remaining time in this house making out with his longtime lovers, self-pity and dejection, before he ran out of money. He had just lost his career, had nobody to blame for it but himself, and was unhirable in any professional industry now. He had every reason to spend time with them—Barry was on a short, clear path to homelessness.

Barry showered.

He fetched the milkshakes and bags of deep-fried sponsored fast food from his porch.

Then he stared out the window as he ate.

Minutes later, the floaters started to gather. Barry opened another document and prepared his fingers for another typing marathon.

I I

Barry had just finished another rousing speech about the will of the light and how it obviously doesn't want to be understood. Sweat dripped from every pore on his body as if he had just ridden the Tour de France on a unicycle. He looked in the mirror.

He had a six-pack. It hadn't been there this morning. At first he was afraid to touch it for fear he might scare it away, but eventually he brought his hand down to his stomach and felt himself. It was real.

The marathon had lasted two solid weeks. Wake up, eat the new meals Platform ordered for him, let his floaters gather, transcribe their debates, shake them up, edit the speeches, and then test what he just wrote.

He was less than half the man he used to be. None of his clothes fit anymore, and for four days he hadn't worn any at all. In years past he didn't like looking at himself naked in the mirror, but now he stared as if gazing at a holy relic.

The transformation had been incredible. He was 170 Platform Weight Units. Thin... Just like the people on streams he admired. He'd always been told it was impossible—no human being had made it below 290 in a century, but here he was! He was energetic, he was alive, and his long-time lovers were nowhere to be found! He didn't feel like spending time with them anymore because for the first time in years he was accomplishing something, and it made him feel good. He got to see progress right before his eyes. Every day he looked at himself before a speech. Then he looked at himself immediately after and saw noticeable difference every time. He had wanted to update his Platform status to *losingweight*, but it had no such status. His routine shower-thought posts were met with absolute silence. No likes. No shares. Nothing. The algorithm didn't show anyone these updates, probably because nobody had ever liked or shared such a post in the past.

Barry pulled himself away and showered. His eye floaters had debated this so many times and in so many different ways Barry wondered how they could possibly continue. Lately he began to wonder when the election would be. He wished he could vote, because he was very much a fan of the voice of reason. Most of his points fit nicely within Barry's character limit. The debates themselves went so far over as to be incomprehensible but full of energy nonetheless. Though the charismatic one was better at igniting the floaters' spirits, the voice of reason was right, and Barry wished he could tell them so.

He turned off the water and returned to the living room. He grabbed one side of the kiddy pool and dragged it to his patio door. Barry slid it through the door, upended the thing into the yard and dumped out the brine.

There had been quite a learning curve. The first thing he noticed was that laying towels on the floor was not enough to absorb the enormous amount of sweat.

He thought about buying tarp, but then he noticed the kiddy pool in his neighbor's yard. It hadn't been used in years except as a breeding area for mosquitoes. After the second speech, Barry drained out all water and larvae and dragged it back inside. There he cleaned it, set it in his living room, and stood in it to give his next speech.

He left the pool on the porch to dry, and then slipped back inside. He took one of his suits from his dresser. It was ten sizes too big for him now. He held it up to his body. It didn't seem real. Two of him could fit in the pants now.

He ran to the computer. He had seventeen speeches, all of them around a hundred pages long and broken into paragraphs only for the purpose of keeping a place.

On the second day, Barry had set up his webcam to record himself performing the speech. He pulled up the video again and sped up the playback five times. He watched himself lose weight. It was visible. It was in real-time! Barry hadn't felt this way since he was a kid sneaking off to gas stations to look at Birds & Blooms magazines that happened to be out of the wrapper.

He then opened his pictures folder. He had been taking stills of himself since the second day. The line of progression was incredible. Day by day Barry became thinner and thinner. All that was missing was a picture for today. He opened the webcam, stepped back while the timer counted down, and snapped another body shot. That shot lined up next to the others on screen.

Barry sat down on the chair and stared at the time-line, mouth agape. His depth of field zoomed inward and focused on his eye floaters. They were gathering again. The soup was thicker than ever in both eyes, but only the ones in the right eye held debates and revered the light.

He glanced at the kiddy pool outside. He looked at his progress shots and the video. He flipped through the speeches. He just realized he hadn't updated his Platform status in days. Most of the milkshakes had gone to waste, and he didn't feel bad about that.

12

Barry sat in front of the smartwall. He had been watching his Profile's streaming feed all day. Platform showed him videos of influencers talking about innovative power tools with men saying things like "plastic tools—scientifically proven just as durable as metal!"

Three videos for do-it-yourself body fluid replacement kits, all with the disclaimer *consult your mechanic before use.* This product brought to you by the Ripauf company. Ripauf: quality ideas meet cost-effective manufacturing.

Three influencers had sponsorship deals with one vacuum cleaner/steam mop/chemistry set/video game console unit. "This one product replaces all these appliances!" Musical pause, allowing for character limit reset. "Now you'll get more done and feel rejuvenated!"

Two ads were for pills or mental exercises guaranteed to increase a person's natural character limit. "You could double your limit!"

The other ten videos were weightloss and exercise programs:

"...diet of bacon grease, and my audiobook will show you how!"

"...potato chip diet! Proven by clinical! How amazing is that?"

"...Indulge with Lipidiamalismi." A barrage of cutaway clips from movies and streaming shows. "Eat what you want, deal with consequences later."

Announcer: "Do you suffer from unsightly belly fat?"

An unnaturally thin woman, obviously computer animated, appeared on the screen: "My belly fat was so unsightly I didn't want to leave my house."

Announcer: "Have you tried diet and just can't seem to lose the weight?" Musical pause. Character limit reset. "Like our profile to let Platform know you want to try..."

Another influencer video had the following ad: A different, unnaturally thin, computer animated woman cut onto the screen saying "I tried everything, but exercise and nutrition are just inco..." She gestured vaguely, trusting the audience knew what she meant.

Platform's stream selected the next video for him. Actually paying attention instead of letting the algorithm pick and then staring mindlessly at the wall for hours and hours was a whole new experience for Barry.

Announcer: "Then why not try Shrink++?! Shrink++ is different!" Animated mascots danced for a solid minute, covering up the character limit reset. "Exercise attacks the fat cells, which are stubborn!" A montage of cutaway quotes from interviews and testimonials about how difficult weightloss is. "Shrink++ works by reducing bone mass, helping you to..."

Unnaturally thin, computer animated woman #3: "It took the weight off! Look at me now! I look virtually..." She gestured to herself.

Unnaturally thin, computer animated woman #4: "I feel rejuvenated!"

Barry checked his notes. Ten different weightloss programs, all of which were either based on lies or half-truths. It seemed everyone wanted to lose weight but common sense and every Platform influencer out there held that it was impossible. Barry had found a way, and he could prove it within the character limit.

For nearly two months he had waited for calls from employers. He was reaching the end of his emergency money. Since he graduated high school full of hope about his future, he thought he finally saw a way to take control of his life.

His first instinct was to start a Platform streaming channel of his own and attempt to become an influencer, but then he thought about the vast ocean of videos already out there, addressing this exact topic. Only the angriest, most outrageous people became influencers, and Barry had no confidence he could stand out.

He had another idea.

It was nearly 4 in the afternoon now, and Barry checked the website of the team-building seminars his former employer used to help its cube-dwellers build relationships and connections. He could demonstrate his weightloss program directly, in person, to hundreds of people, and if he pulled the right strings, he could get an office or two to *require their cube-dwellers to attend his panel as part of a team-building exercise.* He called their information number. It rang five times before someone picked up.

13

Barry didn't have the money to buy new clothes for this meeting, so he walked through the hallway in a baggy shirt, baggy suit jacket, and pants that were now so big on him he could use them to shelter a family of possums.

In one arm he carried his briefcase and the kiddy pool he stole from his neighbor's yard. In the other he held his pants up, bunching up a fistful of fabric and pinching them around his hips as he walked. He considered hemming the waist, or wearing a belt or something, but he figured nothing would look more fake than a man in perfectly fitted clothes pitching a weightloss program to office workers.

Barry was surprised he didn't have to wait when he arrived. The secretary pointed him to the last office, six doors down the hall. Barry had a hard time squeezing his kiddy pool through such a narrow corridor, and he was sure if he hadn't lost all that weight he would not be able to fit at all.

The sixth office down this hall was at the end. The nameplate read: Howard Upvote, Director of Programming. Barry knocked on the door.

"Come in, come in," said a jovial voice. It told Barry that Mr. Upvote was far enough above actual work to be important, a good sign he was talking to someone who actually could make a difference.

Barry slipped inside. Mr. Upvote looked to be at least 340 Platform Weight Units. He stared at Barry's kiddy pool and his loose clothing as he hoisted himself out of the chair and stretched his hand over the desk.

"Mr. Doubletap, I presume?"

Barry shook his hand. "Yes, and I have something incredible to show you!"

"I remember you. You worked for one of my biggest clients."

Barry smiled and nodded as he set the pool on the floor. "They were fond of the escape rooms."

"I remember your name. P&P Auditor. You and 10 others."

"Pirate-themed escape scenarios. Those were my favorites."

Mr. Upvote nodded, glancing at the pool with a raised eyebrow. "My secretary said you are now *independent*."

"Yes, I am."

"And you want to offer a panel for your former employer?"

"Yes, sir," Barry said, setting the kiddy pool down on the floor and the briefcase on the programming director's desk. "They need something besides pirate escape rooms!"

"Mr. Doubletap," Mr. Upvote said, sitting back down. "The only reason I agreed to this meeting is your..."

He gestured vaguely to the phone on his desk as he hit his character limit. Barry noticed the email he sent his secretary on it, showing the videos he had sent of him slimming down in real-time. Clearly he was not in the mood for business interactions, so Barry kept it simple.

"Sir, after I demonstrate, you will want to convince my former..."

Barry felt the ping in his head which told him his brain was out of space. He gestured vaguely in the direction of the city. He trusted Mr. Upvote understood Barry wanted him to convince his former employer to switch from pirate-themed escape rooms to this.

Howard Upvote leaned back in his chair. "Well, I have never seen a person so thin in person, so per..." He gestured toward the pool.

Barry held the waistline of his pants outward. "This is not greenscreen."

"You sound professional. You have ten minutes."

Barry smiled. "Sir, this pool isn't for me. It's for you."

"Come again?"

Barry set his briefcase on the desk and took out his phone. "Are these smartwalls?"

"Yes, they are."

"May I interface?"

Mr. Upvote looked uncertain for a moment, but then he gave Barry the passcode. Barry selected the rear wall, as it had the fewest obstructions. He opened the Platformpoint presentation, and the text "speech 1" appeared on the wall.

Barry then removed his bathroom scale from the briefcase and set it on the floor. He lined up the kiddy pool dead center facing the slide. Mr. Upvote leaned forward and peered over his desk to see what Barry was doing.

"Mr. Upvote," Barry said, pausing to let both of their character limits reset. "As part of my demonstration, please stand on the scale."

Mr. Upvote reluctantly got out of his manager chair. "Mr. Doubletap?"

"I want you to see for yourself. Don't worry, I won't look, *at this time.*" Barry added that last phrase to show he could communicate in a business atmosphere.

Mr. Upvote recognized the character overflow. He waddled around his desk and up to Barry's scale. Barry turned his head away as Mr. Upvote stepped on the scale.

"Remember that number, sir," Barry said. "In a few minutes, it will look a lot better."

He stepped off the scale, and Barry directed him to stand in the kiddy pool, facing the projection.

"All right, sir," Barry said, walking around his desk and reaching over the director's chair for his phone. "All I want you to do is begin reading what appears on the screen."

"What is this supposed to show?"

"Once you get started, you won't be able to stop.."

"All right. Begin the process at this time, Mr. Doubletap. My schedule is diverse and inclusive, keeping me proactively busy."

Businessspeak in return. This was a professional meeting. Barry started the slideshow presentation, set to advance one slide every couple of seconds, but Barry was ready to advance the slides manually if he needed to.

"Light," Mr. Upvote stuttered, staring at the block of text on the wall. "Think about it, fellow employees. We... see it. We know it's there. We bask in it we float in it we adore it we need it to survive. But how many of us stop to look at it?"

Mr. Upvote started out slow and unsure. Gradually the words began to carry him.

"When you look into light, do you see anything? No! We see but we don't even know what we're looking at! We choose to bask in it for hours at a time, days at a time, weeks! We simply float in it, letting it carry us forth from here to there and we never question why!"

Barry smiled and discreetly shook his head. The risk paid off. These speeches didn't have that effect on just him. The director was starting to shout.

"WHY!? WHY?! I ask you to think about this! Why is the light!? Why is the light?! Say it with me, friends, why is the light!? WHY IS THE LIGHT!? WHY! WHY! THE LIGHT!"

Mr. Upvote's arms were getting involved now. He was shaking his fists at the wall, screaming his lungs out. Sweat beaded up and rolled off his expensive suit, collecting in the pool. Ten minutes turned into half an hour, and Mr. Upvote was completely hypnotized and caught up in the momentum. He performed the whole thing, seemingly in a single breath.

When the speech ended, Mr. Upvote stood ankle deep in his own sweat, panting and wheezing, arms still raised. As Barry expected, Platform's microphones detected Mr. Upvote had been doing very stressful yelling, perhaps at a subordinate, so it had ordered him a beverage. A delivery drone tapped on the window, a cup of bubble tea in its claws. Barry opened the window and let the drone fly in, deposit the cup on the desk, and then zip back out.

Mr. Upvote noticed the movement from the corner of his eye, suddenly became aware of himself, took the cup and practically inhaled it. He then righted himself and stared at Barry.

"What in the name of Platform's Founder was that?"

"Step on the scale, sir. See how much progress you made."

Mr. Upvote stepped out of the pool. His pants slipped off his waist and down both legs. Barry caught him before he fell over and hit his head on the desk. He then pulled his feet and pants out of the pool and stumbled in wet feet onto the scale. Barry discreetly turned away from the numbers.

"I... You didn't touch this scale?"

"I didn't, sir."

"I lost twenty PWU. Oh... My pants. My shirt. How is this... Shareholders, proactive, process-driven..."

Certain he could stand on his own, Barry let go of the man's arm. "It's quite intense, isn't it? It does something to you."

Mr. Upvote, still standing on the scale, looked at Barry in wonder. "A weightloss method that works. It's never been done before!"

Barry smiled wide, nodding.

14

Barry peeked through a tiny crack in the collapsible room divider. For a solid minute he strained to focus his vision through the eye floater soup. Finally the next room came into view. Twenty people stood in the auditorium, all of them at least 320 PWU and chatting amongst themselves. Barry could make out snippets of conversation.

"Don't know why I'm here."

"Barry Doubletap? Anyone ever hear of this guy?"

"I wanted the pirate escape room. Why'd we get stuck doing...? Uh... yeah, you know."

"Why do we have to stand in these things?"

Lots of people had come to the seminar. They had no choice. Their bosses required them to go to team-building events like this. True to his word, Mr. Upvote had managed to convince one of the established clients to switch from standard escape rooms and climbing walls and laser tag to Barry's panel instead.

These were technology professionals, all wearing suits or dress shirts. Barry smirked. Everyone stood a small distance apart in their individual kiddy pool. Some were shaped and colored like turtles. Others like kittens. A few were fish-shaped. Others were Sponge Boy, Tiny Mermaid, and other knockoff characters.

Barry backed away from the divider and paced back and forth. This was it. The test to see if it could work. While the programming director had been delirious from exhaustion, Barry had taken a chance and asked if the convention could spare a little loose change to assist him for a few extra kiddy pools and some money for a costume. Perhaps too amazed to say no, Mr. Upvote transferred some Platcoins to his account to buy what he needed with four days to prepare.

He couldn't believe he was now on the other side of the team-building seminars, running one of them, on staff.

With just five minutes until the start of his program, Barry got himself ready to reveal this to a captive audience. He paced back and forth backstage, trying to breathe, trying to remind himself this will work. It had actually been more challenging dealing with his Platform profile this whole time. Platform had no status updates for things like this, and every single one of his posts went by without a single interaction. The sight of his thoughts going unnoticed brought his mood down.

The strange part was how Platform had stopped ordering ice cream shakes and mugs of coffee-flavored creamer for him. He guessed Platform had detected the previous twenty had gone to waste. Barry had been doing something he hadn't done in a long, long, long time: he drank water from the tap. It tasted weird, but he had been desperate.

It was only over this past week he realized he had no way to order food himself, or even make it. The algorithm normally did all of these things for him, so how was he supposed to tell the algorithm something? That's not how technology worked.

Platform had no way to express any of these things. Everything that was happening had no status update to select. He couldn't tell Platform he wanted another shake, and it wasn't ordering him anything usual anymore, so he'd had to adapt to these dramatic circumstances. All of this only added to the anxiety of the moment.

Barry waited until one minute to the top of the hour, and then he steeled himself and stepped through the curtain.

He was dressed like an orchestra conductor: black tuxedo with waistcoat, coattails, and bowtie. His hair was slicked back and combed to one side, hopefully giving him a dignified appearance. He walked out onto the stage with a theatrical air, approached front and center, and took a bow. The audience applauded politely, but they still had no idea what was happening. He heard whispers which showed some were more astonished seeing a thin man in person.

Barry straightened up and clapped his hands together, holding them to his chest. He had rehearsed this a hundred times.

"Good afternoon. I am Barry Doubletap, and at this time, I will proactively serve as your conductor!" He laughed theatrically. "No, no, dear me, no. I am not a conductor of music. I..." Dramatic pause to cover a character limit reset. "...am a conductor of weightloss! Follow my lead."

Barry bowed again, made a precise turn on one heel, and walked to the podium at stage right. He picked up the baton and tapped the stand. That was the cue to the convention staff backstage to lower the smartwall screen. The lights dimmed, the rear door closed, and Barry shook his head to stir up his floaters. To the audience it looked like he was preparing for strenuous activity.

"Begin reading aloud what you see. I will be your guide."

Barry reached down and tapped his phone, starting the slideshow. The text of the speech appeared on the screen. A few people in the audience began reading it, slowly, uncertainly.

> "Light. Light. Look up at it. Look at the light, all of you! Feel it! Bask in it! We all know how we feel when we do, and since time began it is all we needed!"

Barry waved the baton to match their reading pace. The slide advanced automatically. Barry could adjust the rate if needed, but he expected the rate he had chosen would work perfectly.

> "All we needed to be happy was to bask in it, accept it, live in it, float in it, allow ourselves to become it! How does it make you feel?! Let

me hear you! How does it make you feel!"

Their pace quickened. Barry rhythmically waved the baton a little faster in response.

"That's right! That's right! Amen! Amen, it makes you feel happy, content and satisfied! Then I ask you what happens when you try to discern the light?!"

The attendees became synchronized as they shouted, pumping their arms, stamping their feet, waving their hands around, but none strayed from their pools. The noise reverberated against the walls and heated the air. Barry pretended to conduct them, making it appear as though he were in control, but Barry merely reacted to them. When they picked up the pace, Barry waved the baton faster. When the audience hit an intense spot in the speech, Barry acted more aggressive, as if driving the orchestra forward and squeezing passion from their very souls.

Barry kept it up for a solid hour. The kiddy pools filled. The people standing in them sloshed around. Pants fell into the pools of sweat, and the people kept orating. There was just something primally stimulating about these speeches—no matter what kind of person you were, you couldn't hold back. To see an entire group of people falling into it was creepy. For a few moments, while Barry waved the baton around to the cadence, he felt as if he really was in control.

The speech ended. Everyone in the audience stood in a pool of their own sweat, pants fallen around their ankles, shirts hanging looser than they had before. They stared at Barry, some with their arms still in the air, as if expecting him to do something.

Barry casually set the baton back on the stand and strode to the center of the stage. He spread his arms. The audience members looked at themselves. They didn't even reach for their pants.

"Give yourselves a hand! You are the performance! What a diverse group of people you are! You are proactive! You create value for shareholders! Thank you! Thank you!"

They applauded. Louder and louder.

"Take a bow!" Barry shouted.

The audience bowed to him.

"A fantastic performance! Absolutely fantastic!"

One by one they picked up their feet and walked out the door. Many lost their balance, not used to carrying less weight around. Seminar staff caught the people and handed out towels for their feet and sweat-laden faces.

Barry quietly slipped behind the curtain and took a few deep breaths. He saw movement from the corner of his eye. Mr. Upvote was standing off to the side.

"Well done, Barry," he said. "I think you made an impression on them."

"Did you see their faces when they looked at themselves?"

Mr. Upvote laid a hand on his shoulder. "I lined up another captive audience of cube-dwellers."

"Really?"

"Tomorrow. I have a feeling you'll go far."

Barry was still catching his breath. "Thank you. I'll do it. Just tell me when."

"Same time," he said, turning to go. "By the way, nice outfit. Conductor of Weightloss. I like it at this time. Shareholder value."

"Thanks. See you tomorrow."

Mr. Upvote exited through one of the side doors. Barry was suddenly hit by ten rapid flashes to the brain and almost dropped to the floor from pain and shock. Then shouts and cheers erupted from his right eye.

> "Thank you! Thank you all! Thank you for electing me! I promise together we will understand the light! No longer will we be content to bask and float! From now on, we will learn! We will reason! We will quantify and comprehend!"

The floaters were jumping up and down and leaping from one side of his retina to the other in jubilation. His right eye flashed and sparked a thousand times in under a minute as the voice of reason spoke over the din.

> "Today you have chosen change! You have chosen truth! You are wonderful! We are wonderful! We will seek the light! We will seek it!"
>
> —*flashflashflashflash*—

"Seek!"

—*flashflashflashflash*—

"SEEK!"

—*flashflashflashflashflash-flashflash*—

"SEEK THE LIGHT!"

—*FLASH—FLASH—SPARK*—

"WE WILL SEEK EVERY-THING IN THE LIGHT!"

The fireworks brought Barry to the floor, clutching his skull. He wanted to shake his floaters apart, but the flashes were so bright he couldn't convince his muscles to coordinate that much.

I 5

Barry stood at the podium, waving his baton, pretending to conduct the audience while they shouted in synchronization.

"The answer lies not in acting on behalf of the light, but understanding it! For far too long that's what we have been content to do! Float and bask and forget, believing we know what the light wants just by doing so, but no more! We must understand it! We must become it!"

Forty people. The programming director had bought more kiddy pools for Barry's show and got an even larger group of office workers in need of team-building for him. Barry heard what attendees were saying about him. He had walked the convention halls after the show in his performance costume, meeting the people, carrying himself like a stereotypical orchestra conductor.

They asked him questions, wanting to know who he was, where he came from, why this worked. People who had been to the performance said none of the clothes they brought to the seminar fit anymore, and they wanted to know how this was possible. Barry remained theatrical and friendly, never giving direct answers, letting the magic take root in their minds.

Word had definitely gotten around, for now people came in wearing stretchy pants that were one size too small for them to begin with. From this vantage point, Barry could watch them shrink down to fit into these pants in real time.

"That is the only way we will know what it wants! Say it with me! Why is the light! Why is the light! Why! Why! Keep saying it! Keep thinking it at all times and the next time you look at the light and are tempted merely to float and bask in its glory, stop yourself! Look out the window and see the shapes! See the motion! See beyond the sum and look at the parts and understand why!"

Hearing a group of forty people shouting and screaming the same words at the same time was humbling and terrifying. If not for Barry's role as conductor, he wouldn't want to be anywhere near so much uncontained, savage energy.

> "Why! The most important question is why! Why opens our minds to new possibilities! Now is the time to understand the parts of the whole, and in doing so we will gain knowledge of our place therein! No more floating! No more basking! We will understand!"

Their faces were so red they looked ready to burst. Veins stood out. Sweat poured from their skin and flowed down their saturated clothes and into the pools.

The speech went on. Nearly an hour of concentrated, unfocused energy. Barry's conducting matched their passion and he figured he was losing enough calories just playing this role now. Not nearly as much as the people performing the speeches on the projector, but enough to keep him at his present weight, which was a source of fascination for all who met him. It was just as well. His conductor costume was the only set of clothes that fit him now, and nobody sold clothes for people of this frame unless they were for mannequins.

The act of conducting and swinging his body to and fro and side to side kept his floaters stirred up. They gathered only during his downtime, so he didn't have to keep them broken up anymore. He barely noticed them now, occupied as he was by the show.

Barry kept waving the baton while the audience performed a symphony of light and understanding. When it was over, Barry crossed his arms before him and cut outwards, as if ordering the orchestra to halt. The audience became still. Only the sound of dripping sweat filled the room. He then gently placed the baton on the podium, walked to the center of the stage, and applauded.

The audience stood in place, looking themselves over, panting and wheezing and coughing and marveling that they now fit the smaller pants. Then they applauded with Barry. Again, Barry announced that he didn't deserve any applause. It was they, the audience, the performers, who deserved it. He slipped backstage.

Barry heard people sloshing out of sweat pools, toweling themselves off, marveling at the results. Barry sat and recomposed himself, taking several long drinks. When he had calmed down enough to channel the spirit of David Niven again, he exited the theater and walked the convention, shaking hands and answering questions with cool, theatrical dignity. It turned into an informal Q and A session in the convention center hallway. Barry stood there and answered questions for more than an hour before removing a fake pocket watch from his waistcoat and announcing it was time to take his leave.

Barry quietly slipped into one of the restrooms. He had stashed a change of clothes here earlier in the day. Cheap clothes purchased with the con money that he had sewn large foam plates underneath to make him look normal so he wouldn't be recognized out of character. He quickly switched them out, making sure his foam belly and thighs and sagging underarms were firmly in place, and then opened the door and came face to face with Mr. Upvote. Barry jumped back, startled.

"Second good show, Barry. This is no fluke."

"Thanks for your help."

Mr. Upvote looked him up and down. "Nice disguise. Now what?"

"Scheduling. I have offers for other team-building seminars."

Mr. Upvote smiled. "I've had 50 calls from clients asking for more info on you."

Barry's mind traveled around the world 8 times in less than a second and then returned to take control of Barry's mouth like so: "Good! Nobody can get noticed on Platform anymore so this is..." He gestured vaguely.

Mr. Upvote snorted. "Who'd have thought something off Platform would get noticed."

Barry smiled, happy they understood one another without businessspeak formalities.

Mr. Upvote's character limit had emptied and was ready again. "What's your fee at this present time?"

Businessspeak before a character limit. That got Barry's attention. "My fee?"

The programming director laughed. "You do intend to make money this way, correct?"

"Oh, yes, of course. Uh, what's typical?"

Mr. Upvote whispered it in Barry's ear.

"That's what my rate will be then!" Barry said, shaking Mr. Upvote's hand.

"I'll be in touch for booking clients. Since I gave you a proactive first chance, how about a discounted rate, at this time?" Mr. Upvote smiled.

"I promise! Thank you so much for this!"

"Good luck out there." He turned to leave, then stopped himself, looked over his shoulder and said, "Oh, and you may keep the pools."

Mr. Upvote left the restroom. Barry followed a few minutes later, after he had processed the moment. In his baggy clothes and foam pads, he looked like a normal person instead of a freak who had actually lost weight. Nobody recognized him, and he was glad for that. He walked to his car, tucked his costume under the seat, and caught his breath in the driver's seat.

Barry helped the con staff clean up the pools and deflate them. Then he loaded everything in his vehicle. He didn't want the rest of the staff to know who he was for fear that seeing him out of character and costume would ruin the magic. He simply told them that Mr. Upvote said he should take the pools with him, and they asked no questions. All forty of them fit in his car with much squeezing.

He drove home and crashed on the couch. His phone rang, and Barry answered, pretending to be Mr. Doubletap's secretary. He spent the next four hours coordinating a schedule of tradeshow and business seminar appearances, ranging from next week to next month.

Late at night, Barry recorded a new voicemail and set the phone to go directly to that. He sat on his living room couch, facing a blank wall. His house hadn't switched on and displayed his Platform feed.

Silence. Silence. Peace.

Just as he began to wonder why, a tiny voice of reason rose from within.

> "Have you been keeping up your observations?"

> Various low-toned shouts in the affirmative responded.

> "Good, good, that's good. How many of you were unable to resist the temptation to bask and float?"

> A good many sheepishly responded in the affirmative.

> "I understand. I, too, fell into temptation frequently since we were last able to come together. I want to share with you my observations so far, while we have this moment of calm and nothing is stirring us up."

Barry smiled while he watched his floaters gather. He relocated to the computer and opened a new document.

> "They are out there!" began the voice of reason. "Shapes are everywhere! Movement! Movement as I could never discern before, but the longer I observe, the clearer they become. I see things moving about, but not as we

move. They move in straight lines, side to side, not up and down as we know it. And what's more, these movements sometimes cease! They stand still!"

Many floaters voiced that they have observed the same things.

"Still! Imagine what that must be like! Standing still! Holding still! Not subject to the whims and motions of the current, but able to stand still. Comrades! We can learn from this! If they can hold still, why can't we? Why can't we come up with some kind of way to hold ourselves still? Think about it! If we were not at the mercy of the motion, we could observe and discern the light easier."

The floaters voiced two different opinions. Some wanted to keep basking and didn't like the idea that this one was proposing an end to that.

"I'm not saying we shouldn't bask, comrades! This is merely an observation of what's going on outside the window. Things stand still! They move when they want to move, not just when the current moves them. We should do the same thing because movement is our joy! We must control our movement!"

The floaters agreed and started waving their webby limbs

around, rocketing around where they wanted to go as a show of it.

"Movement! Movement! Movement! MOVEMENT!" repeated the voice of reason as the floaters moved around him, on their own. "That's right! There is much to learn observing the light, and in the light we have seen things that don't move! Things that control their motion and don't allow themselves to be caught up in the current and swirled about! Why should we be any different? So remember this! Remember this and control your movement! Bask when you want to, not just when the current catches you, but when you choose it! We have all seen it in the light and as the light does, so should we!"

"Control!" answered the congregation.

"Yes, control!" echoed the voice of reason. Barry wondered where the charismatic one was these days.

"Control!" the audience and the voice of reason chanted over and over.

The speech went on for an hour, and Barry typed it out. When he'd had enough, Barry shook his head a little.

"This is it! Don't give in to the current! Push against it! Control your movement!"

Some of the floaters tried, but in the end they couldn't seem to resist being caught up in the flow. The floaters went motionless, and the voices stopped.

Barry smiled and uploaded the new speech into his master folder. As he did, he looked around at the blank walls. Still no Platform feed. No shakes delivered to his front door. No fast food. He had gotten by at the seminar taking food from other people's drone deliveries, just a piece or a sip or two here and there, fun gestures of a busy seminar atmosphere, but for Barry it had been foraging. Platform, it seemed, had forgotten about him, and Barry now sat down and opened his profile. He did something he had never done before: he looked at restaurants and other things in the area, and decided for himself what he wanted to eat. Telling Platform he wanted to do something felt weird, and the function was buried so far into the settings he never would have found it had he not been looking for it.

Barry ordered his own meal. When it arrived minutes later, double deep-fried burgers and a coffee-flavored ice cream shake, he sat down and looked at the blank walls again.

He took a sip of the shake.

It was so thick.

Too sweet.

Barry couldn't remember ever regarding something as too sweet before.

The burgers were too greasy.

Not only had Platform abandoned him, but he couldn't seem to enjoy the basics anymore either.

16

He had booked himself one business seminar or tradeshow per weekend over the next several months. For those first few appearances, he would have had to book his own hotel rooms, but he couldn't justify the expense, so he parked a couple lots over and slept in his car, hoping nobody would notice.

Platform had no status update for *sleeping in my car*. Barry had never felt more alone.

In the second month, Barry received a room courtesy of every tradeshow, which made life so much easier.

By now Barry had enough money to buy a real outfit suitable for an orchestra conductor. No more costume, no more fake baton. Now he had the real thing, sewn and cinched up to fit his frame properly, no foam pieces. Since Platform influencers were starting to talk about him on their channels, he figured it was a good idea to make sure everything stood up to scrutiny; if something did not, he was sure to hear about it endlessly.

Influencers often speculated about where he got his idea, and why these speeches had such an impact. Most videos and commentary had to do with what the speeches meant. Lots and lots and lots of people who had no experience speaking outside their character limit trying to understand what the floaters were saying. They couldn't parse a single sentence of the text, so they resorted to gestures and vague speculation.

Other people hyping him up was the best thing he could have hoped for—he never would have become famous putting himself out there online in the ocean of reaction videos and news commentary and movie reviews and trailer reactions and reactions to trailer reaction videos and preliminary pre-announcements for this and that, and the commentary videos reaction to the pre-reaction commentaries and reviews.

His floaters were becoming more and more difficult to keep apart. Barry got the feeling that even when they were drifting, they were active. Barry didn't like it, but with the overhead of cross-country travel and so much time devoted to seminar preparation there simply wasn't enough time to deal with it.

His compensation for helping cube-dwellers and managers and field techs and executives build a team spirit through a shared experience was substantial. Money flowed in, but he wasn't swimming in it. Barry didn't blow the money on anything. He saved like crazy for the inevitable body maintenance procedures.

Multiple times Barry lay alone in his hotel room, staring at the ceiling, marveling that he was making a living doing this. Yes, it had happened. Only when he thought about it did he consider it might be temporary.

It's too good to be true. It can't last. Thoughts like these were only in his peripheral consciousness. Right now, he enjoyed being a conductor of businessspeak instead of spewing it out every day. He deserved this. It would last.

His next tradeshow was on the other side of the country. This was a convention of restaurant owners. Other events on the schedule included guest speakers presenting "tips on how to pay less and expect more." These were the most common topics for managers at such business gatherings: ways to convince people that accepting less pay for more work was in fact a virtue and a service to the public.

After a long drive and another difficult time helping the staff set up while wearing his foam disguise, Barry entered from stage left, gave his usual opening address, and then took his place behind the podium. He raised the baton, and a projector screen lowered. The lights dimmed. The text appeared on the smartwall, and Barry began conducting.

Forty people dressed in clothes one size too small for them, standing in brightly colored kiddy pools, began reading. Barry didn't even have to instruct them anymore. Word had spread of the procedure.

Thirty seconds passed.

The audience wasn't getting caught up in the energy of the speech. They read it in pure monotone, waiting for something amazing to happen, but nothing was. They began to look at one another for confirmation that it wasn't just them.

After a minute, Barry lowered the baton and tapped the podium, reaching down and halting the Platformpoint presentation. The text stopped, and the audience turned to him. Barry maintained the dignified smile. In the one second of silence between Barry tapping the baton for attention and his next words, his conscious mind left his body, circled the earth seventeen times, then altered trajectory to intercept his skull again and fill his mouth with something.

"Oh my, this one failed to engage. Have you seen it before?" Barry raised his hand, indicating the audience members should do the same to answer in the affirmative.

Forty hands raised.

"Ah, I believe that may be our problem. Gentlemen," Barry said to the open air. "Ninth speech."

He reached down to his phone and loaded a different slideshow into Platformpoint.

"Thank you, sirs," Barry bowed slightly, raised the baton and his hand. "Now, let's try again."

He flicked his wrists and waved the baton. The audience began reading. In less than ten seconds, Barry felt energy rushing at him. Better. Much better. Within the hour, the pools filled up, tight clothes became fitted, and the people applauded Barry as he applauded them.

Backstage, while Barry took a drink from the fountain, he pondered what just happened. He almost blew a show. If not for his quick thinking, the whole thing would've fallen apart and his reputation would have been smeared.

He had bumped up against a limit: the same speech wouldn't work on a person twice. Barry silently branched thought processes off of this. It was a good thing. He knew this now, so it wouldn't catch him off guard next time. He would simply have to start promoting which speech he was going to present ahead of time and warn people not to come if they had heard it before.

It made sense. Now that word was starting to get around in person and across Platform, there were bound to be repeats. Now he knew...

Barry gradually became aware of activity in his vitreous humor.

> "Fellow comrades!" shouted the voice of reason. "Have you been observing, as I have?"
>
> Many affirmative shouts.
>
> "You have not merely been basking?"
>
> Many negative shouts.
>
> "You have not allowed the momentum of the fluid and the warmth of the light to cloud your minds?"
>
> Louder negative shouts.
>
> "Good, comrades, then you will already know what I am about to tell you. Or if you don't know, you will at least have an inkling of it. Things are moving in the light all the time. Things moving to and fro, here to there. All of these things are darker than the light. It leads me to believe they are not of the light."

The crowd murmured. Barry straightened up and walked to the staging area. He was going to break them up, but something told him he should listen this time.

> "That's right! What's outside the window is not merely light! It's not just where the light

comes from! There is a more out there! A place where things do not move like we do, do not look like we do, do not act like we do. The light is there, too, we merely catch what comes in the window. That's right! That's what I'm saying! The light does not exist solely for us! It doesn't shine only to give us life! It gives life to the outside as well! I know what you're thinking. I know what you're saying. Life. Out there. Life that is not like us. Yes, comrades. There is more life on the outside. There is more life beyond us. Therefore I ask you to consider: where are we?"

Barry shook his head. His floaters swirled around before his eye. The soup was thicker now than ever. His vision had become cloudier. Things that were once white were now just a few shades away from totally black.

"Where are we, comrades?! Focus your observations and share them with one another until next we meet! Observe! Don't bask! Seek the light, and now I urge you to seek what's beyond the light! Seek!"

"SEEK!"

"Seek!"

"SEEK!"

They repeated this several times and then the voices died off. His floaters now floated around in his vision. Barry struggled to find a slightly less-dense area through which to focus.

Barry realized he couldn't go to Flui-X-Change now. He only had eighteen speeches, which wouldn't carry this for long. He needed his floaters just as they were.

Barry composed himself, slipped into character again. He worked the convention crowd as usual until the early hours of the morning. Finally everyone went to sleep. Barry took his phone out and started typing out what he remembered of the voice of reason's speech earlier.

In no time his floaters gathered again and shared rousing debate over exactly what they were seeing. This speech was different from the ones Barry wrote down in months past. He hoped it would have the same effect. Everything was on the line now.

17

All of the interviews Barry had given so far were on the spot in convention centers, or in the hallways of hotels. The tradeshows and seminars that booked him were not open to the general public, so when influencers and aspiring influencers and critics and commentators snuck in to get footage, they felt like undercover agents, and Barry eagerly took their questions. Usually one or two followed by a brief statement. The influencers didn't seem to like interviewing him because he always gave dignified, uninformative answers. Much more interesting were the people who walked out of his panels, shouting and screaming at their new, lighter figures. Barry preferred it that way. He hoped it would create a mystical perception. The more people who spoke on his behalf, the more professional he would seem. Barry had no way of knowing if this strategy was working, or if he was just plain wrong.

Until now.

Barry sat in a studio under hot overhead lights. His costume had a few extra lights shining on it to help it show up on camera. Barry smiled at that. His costume had special lights devoted to it. He was told without them it would appear as a two-dimensional shape on screens. The lights would give it form and depth. The grips commented they had never lit so thin a person before, so they were winging it and hoping for the best.

Barry was caked in makeup. His face had makeup, his eyes had highlighter, his lashes were done, his eyebrows had been plucked, he was wearing lipstick, then the director told him to "be natural."

The reporter sitting opposite him was blonde and beautiful at 340 Platform Weight Units. She hadn't started out that way. The makeup artists applied her facial beauty, and Barry watched her transform from normal person to television personality in just half an hour. She wore a green suit, and like all streaming personalities, computer animation would be applied in real time to make her appear 99 PWU. Meanwhile, Barry needed no such techniques. His physique was real, except for his face, which had to be made flawless for the cameras.

The reporter faced the camera and read from a teleprompt.

"Thank you for tapping Edgelord Streaming News."

A montage played: a series of two-word clips from previous interviews. The camera switched back to the reporter.

"I have Mr. Barry Doubletap giving his first interview."

Another cutaway montage of previous interviews, no more than three words from the same person. This was how the news was done: a cutaway every sixty characters so the audience could empty their minds and accept the next thought.

"He is known as the Conductor of Weightloss, but who is he?"

Montage number three. Now that Barry thought about it, this was how all streaming shows were structured. All influencer videos. All advertisements. Everything...

"Despite having no Platform presence, he has achieved fame."

Fourth cutaway montage. Barry was getting antsy. He had never noticed just how long it took to get through anything.

Three montages later, she finally turned to face Barry and addressed him directly.

"Mr. Doubletap—do you prefer to be called maestro, conductor?"

"Mr. Doubletap is fine," Barry said, smiling theatrically.

"Mr. Doubletap is it."

She laughed charismatically, and the stream cut to an automated montage of various charismatic laughs plucked from lots and lots of different influencer and streaming news videos.

"Platform is abuzz about you," she resumed. "Who exactly are you?"

Barry gave a dignified chuckle. It was going to be difficult to stick to a character limit without lapsing into businessspeak. "I used to work in an office. I discovered true weightloss... and... you know." He gestured vaguely.

"Everyone says it's impossible. How do you make it possible?"

"I tap into primal energies. People are so passionate..." He made *falling off* gestures with his hands as soon as he hit sixty characters.

The reporter nodded. "People are taking notice of you. How does it make you feel?"

"I see progress happen right before my eyes. It's fantastic."

"It must be very emotional. Please tell us how you felt."

"I feel pretty good. I get to make a difference instead of..." Barry made office-worker gestures.

"We've compiled testimonies. If you would, please."

A stagehand directed him to a monitor to his left, and he watched a montage of cutaways from interviews conducted after his seminars. People who had been to them. People who shared their before and after photos on Platform. People who had themselves recorded at his seminar, and the footage speed up to show weightloss in real time. Six interviews, saying how much his program changed their lives. Influencers reporting on the ground, live-commenting to viewers about the raw energy in the air, the smell of sweat, the passion, the energy, and the visible reduction in mass happening in front of them. Thirty PWU lost. Forty PWU. Sixty. Incredible results, and they all want to know who Barry was. Why this works. Why nobody had thought of it before. The compilation ended, and the cameras focused on Barry and the reporter again.

"How does that make you feel?" she asked him.

"I'm just as amazed."

"And your feelings after watching?"

"Uh, same as before."

"NO FACTS! TELL US HOW YOU FEEL! PEOPLE WANT TO KNOW!"

The reporter's face burst out of her makeup, leaving her less-than-perfect face exposed for everyone to see. She leaned on the table, snarling. Barry cowered in his seat. After a beat of silence, a team surrounded the reporter and reapplied her makeup while adjusting her green suit, and then disappeared behind camera. The interview resumed.

"Let that be your warning. No facts. Just feelings, or else..."

She made ax-murderer gestures.

Barry nodded slowly.

"That part won't be streamed. How did that make you feel?"

"I feel... rewarded that I'm helping so many people," Barry said, regaining his composure on the way.

"Many are asking why you haven't started a Platform channel."

"For now I'm concentrating on in-person experiences."

The reporter glared at him from under her makeup.

Barry's heart fluttered. "Oh, and I feel very enthusiastic about the future."

He shivered a little.

The reporter smiled, retreating back into her makeup.

"People are asking how you came up with this."

"Had to give a speech at work and I lost weight." Before she could threaten him again, Barry added, "I felt alive."

She nodded approvingly underneath her makeup.

Barry answered her next ten questions as best he could. He was honest up to and not including his eye floaters. That was one fact he didn't want to escape. Barry could see them through the entire interview, floating, watching everything. At least they were quiet. Perhaps they liked the studio lights.

"Thank you for choosing Edgelord. How was the experience?"

Barry smiled and laughed theatrically. "I felt intimidated."

The reporter smiled and laughed. The face under her makeup did not look amused. Barry hoped he hadn't crossed the line, but he laughed with her anyway.

He got out of there as fast as possible and dashed back to his hotel room. He took a few deep breaths when he was sure he was alone. He hoped he would never have to do a streaming news service ever again.

His next interview was over the phone with a movie reviewer on Platform, one of the angriest and most vulgar people on the planet, which was the only way to rise to the top on Platform. The interview was just as angry, with a cutaway montage of movie clips every ten seconds, each segment lasting less than one second each.

So many interviews this week. Until now, he had booked himself full every weekend with tradeshow and seminar appearances, but this month there happened to be a week-long gap, so he filled it with interviews.

Interview after interview after interview, with phone calls on top of them to book him for conventions, and he had his floaters to deal with. Between interviews, Barry transcribed their speeches. New debates emerged. These debates were about the meaning of existence. What is life? How can we recognize life? Where are we? Why are we?

Barry had been worried now that they weren't preparing for an election the speeches would become stale, unsuitable for weightloss. While the new speeches were different, they still contained raw exuberance that had to be vocalized. The floaters were just as determined as ever to understand these things that moved around in the light. Apparently as their observations became keener, so did their perception of what was going on outside Barry's eye.

They were now able to make out individual people. They recognized faces. They recognized certain objects now, like computers, phones, bottles, steering wheels, and stoplights. They made note of what happened to the surrounding environment when certain things happened. For example, how everything stopped when the light was red, but began moving again when it turned green. They had no words to describe these things.

On the last day of interviews, the voice of reason made a startling speech. It began with:

> "We have observed common
> features on these objects. We al-
> ways see the same two features.

White globes with circles in the center, over which a cover flicks closed and then opens periodically. Does this seem familiar?"

Affirmative shouts and hollers. Barry typed furiously.

"Our realm is the same way. We live in a spherical realm—multiple surveys have confirmed this—and the light flickers from time to time, so often we barely notice. It is consistent with what we have observed watching creatures on the outside. The shaking. We have observed the creatures moving about. What if our currents and violent motion is the result of this? Comrades... This is huge! We are living components of another life form!"

While he typed, his mind wandered. In all the interviews, questions, and testimonies people wanted to know one thing: why did this work? Why did the speeches have this effect on people? The longer Barry listened to his floaters, the more aware he became of how he didn't understand a thing they said. Nobody did, and influencers on Platform sure tried. Now Barry began to wonder what the floaters were saying.

Could this mean something? Some sort of significance beyond what he could see right now? As every child who grew up using Platform learned, all that mattered was see meme, share meme. Sixty characters was all anyone needed to express anything. More than that was only wasted words. Barry's experience in the business world had confirmed this: all real thought ceased after sixty characters of information. Anything worth expressing only needed that much. His eye floaters seemed to have tapped into something else. Was there more to it beyond its viral appeal on Platform and the money coming in?

Quickly Barry dismissed the thought. He needed speeches, and he needed more money to cover his travel expenses and his routine bodily fluid exchanges, plus his future eye fluid maintenance.

"Keep 'em coming, guys. Barry needs a new pair of eyes," he said as he typed.

His phone rang. Barry thought he had set it to voicemail. Instead of ignoring it, out of pure habit he picked it up.

"Mr. Doubletap's office. How may I direct your call?"

"Yes, I am interested in booking Mr. Doubletap at this time," said a familiar male voice. "Is he available at this time?"

"He isn't available at this time, sir, but I can schedule a diverse booking for late next month if you wish. Shareholders, bottom line, diversity."

"That would be perfect. My colleagues and I would be interested in having him proactively attend our team-building seminar at this time."

Barry's eyebrows rose. He couldn't get over that voice. So familiar, so jovial, so businesslike and yet so aggressive and predatory. He had heard it before, but he couldn't place it.

"I would be happy to schedule Mr. Doubletap to appear," Barry said.

18

Barry walked around in casual clothes padded with foam to blend in. He looked like a professional of Information Technology, or systems networking, or a consultant. He wore a name badge and wandered the halls as if he was supposed to be there.

Barry scanned the crowd, listened for people who seemed familiar. Barry had a feeling he would know people here, though they wouldn't recognize him when they saw him on stage.

He stood in the midst of multiple conversation groups. All across the seminar he heard things like:

"Well at this time we are in the process of adjusting our overhead to align with company specifications."

"We have decided to leverage the overseas labor force in order to better serve our clients today."

"Recently I read an article that stated the best course of action in my company's scenario may be to focus value on tangible resources using robust technology to solve real-world problems and deliver shareholder value, which I plan to do at this time."

"...utilize memory..."

"...abstain from radicalism..."

"...maintain synergy..."

"...define core processes..."

In one of these groups, he spotted her. She was talking to what Barry assumed were her peers.

"...at my previous position I strove to quantify employee appearances and actions to determine if they were aligned with company standards. I feel that I increased shareholder value by as much as ten percent over the time I held that position."

"And how long did you utilize communication to facilitate growth while aligning with company policy and shareholder values in that position?" one of the other men asked.

"I feel that I held it long enough to make a tangible difference. After this I furthered my personal development with my current employer as an assistant to one of my supervisors."

She smiled, laughed, and indicated the man standing next to her. Barry recognized him now. It was the Big Boss, the man who had fired the auditors earlier this year and set Barry on his current path.

While she spoke, the others noticed Barry.

"Alexis Sponsoredcontent," Barry said. "Remember me?"

Alexis paused for a moment of recognition, and then smiled and laughed and gave Barry a nondiscriminatory embrace followed by an inclusive, teambuilding handshake.

"Barry! How have you been?" Her smile was too big to be real.

"It's been tough, but I'm still out there."

"That's wonderful! That's wonderful to hear." She faced the rest of the group, who politely waited to be introduced. "Everyone, this is Barry Doubletap, a proactive former colleague of mine."

Barry shook hands with everyone, then returned to his position in the circle of suited businessspeak.

"Dressed a little unprofessionally at this time, aren't you?" said the Big Boss.

"Actually," Barry said, "You invited me here to give a performance."

"Ah, at this time I see now, diversely!" said the Big Boss. "Barry Doubletap. Please utilize your unique communication skills, at this present time and in the most non-discriminatory manner, to enlighten me how you managed after earning eight citations for violation of company policy."

Barry smiled. For the first time in his life, he had so much to say.

"Yes, you told us to give a presentation to save our jobs from being eliminated. I gave the most unique one, so I was punished extra. If I recall, everybody else, including the former A&A Auditor, was cited four times for violations. What happened, Alexis? You got fired but then Mr. Shame here offered to hire you on for less pay and you took it as a favor?"

Alexis smiled and laughed like a good professional.

"And what happened to the other auditors?" Barry continued. "Corey, Jennifer, Bob, remember them?"

"Bob is managing director of Information Acquisition," said the Big Boss. "At this time I am unsure of the others."

Barry laughed. It wasn't a fake, formal laugh. The others in the group had no idea what to make of it.

"Hiding in a frivolous job. That's us. No useful function. Just eat up payroll and hope nobody notices you're irrelevant. That's how every auditor lived. We hid in the cracks. Wasn't our fault the company finally found the crack and flushed out the infection. I wonder how long it will take before they find the crack you're hiding in."

"I beg your pardon at this time, Barry," said the Big Boss. "We contribute a great deal to our respective, dynamic companies, and to the diverse society. We have proactively overcome societal norms, utilizing technology and personal motivation to achieve shareholder value."

Barry laughed again. "If you took out all the at this times, proactivelys and utilizes, you'd be left with sixty characters of actual thought, and half of those mention shareholders. What's the point of speaking above the limit if you have to fill it with devotion to them, whoever they are? Well, I've found a way to create value for *me*. Nobody else."

The Big Boss puffed his cheeks. Barry didn't know anybody really did that. "Mr. Doubletap! You mean to do more than imply by the words you choose?"

"Yes, I just said things, and I meant what I said!"

"And nothing you said was previously spoken by another person? You utilized your own words at this time?"

"That's right. My own words to mean what I think. For the first time in my life I can say them."

The Big Boss opened his mouth to speak. Then closed it. Then he opened it again. Then closed it.

Barry smiled. "Normal people go to work, update their Platform status, and go home. No imagination. What are you people doing different? I have been so busy I have not opened Platform in months. Platform doesn't pick my meals anymore. It doesn't choose my entertainment. I do. Listen to me now. I'm speaking outside my character limit, and I think I mean what I say. I think... I think I understand what I'm saying."

The Big Boss opened his mouth, and this time something came out. "Uh... yeah..."

Barry smiled. "I'm glad to see Alexis found another crack to hide in. I wasn't so lucky. Nobody would hire me with those citations on my record. So you know what I did? I'm not just hiding in the cracks anymore. I'm doing something useful. It's a three-day seminar, ladies and gentlemen, meant to help you build relationships and team spirit. I hope you'll join me for both panels."

Barry shook hands with everyone. As he walked away, he could hear the men and women trying to understand what he just said. It was so direct, so simple... They couldn't quite wrap their heads around what he meant.

Barry had forgotten what it was like being in a business atmosphere. He'd been used to such direct, fiery talk from his eye floaters he forgot there was an entire existence where people considered it a mark of professional virtue to use as many meaningless words as possible. Barry couldn't believe he'd been part of it for so long. Compared to Barry's eye floaters, the professional, intellectual people were downright empty. His floaters spoke outside the character limit, and it lit a fire in his audience every time. These people spoke outside their character limit, and it left everyone feeling deflated.

As he walked through the convention, Barry pondered what he had just done. He had said meaningful words beyond his own limit. He tried to do it again, but now that he was alone, the feeling was gone. He couldn't summon any thoughts in excess of sixty characters. Couldn't string that many words together without losing the thought. What had happened?

A connection was there. Some kind of significance hidden in all of this. Barry tried to hold onto it for a while, but he lost the thought and started looking forward to earning his appearance fee. He smiled at the thought that the man who had fired him was about to pay him.

19

The smartwall lit up, and Barry tapped the baton on the podium. Eighty people standing in kiddy pools. His biggest audience at his biggest venue yet. All of them were business professionals, and here Barry stood, the only thin person in the room—the only thin person any of them had seen outside of a streaming show—about to conduct them. Barry almost grinned, but maintained his persona and waved the baton as the audience began reading.

"We live in a spherical realm. We have observed many things outside the window, and now we cannot escape the one conclusion we must draw from it. There is more to the sphere than just this! Than just us! We are not the reason the light exists! The light doesn't know who we are, but it shines on everything just the same as it does us! We are not the only form

of life that exists. Let's pon-
der this, comrades! We are
not the only form of life!"

In no time the audience became swept up in the rhetoric. The noise was incredible. Barry had never heard so much energy expelled in so small a space before. It wasn't easy to keep his composure, especially with the audience blowing this much hot air in his direction. Barry worked up a sweat just standing on the stage.

This speech only took 45 minutes to complete, but by the time it was over, not a fitted pair of pants could be seen. In fact, some who had intentionally worn pants one size too small found that even these were too big. Barry had been worried about the speech's effectiveness, as it was just musing on the observations and speculations about life outside the vitreous humor, and what it meant to the eye floaters. It seemed to touch something special inside of everyone here.

Barry took center stage, bowed, and then applauded. While the audience applauded in reply, Barry found the Big Boss, standing in the pool of his own sweat, pants bunched up and floating around his ankles. Barry silently dared the boss to cite him now.

He walked the seminar in character, shaking hands and answering questions with his usual noncommittal formality. He didn't see his former coworkers again, but he didn't need to. He had said everything he wanted to say.

The second show ran without any complications, and this speech was a different speech about the same topic. Barry never ran the same speech twice now, not after that last incident. He didn't want to run the risk of any one person in the audience not being affected, for that would ruin the magic. Every speech was new, and he only had a few weeks worth of lead time before he was completely out of material.

When the seminar concluded, Barry shook hands with many of the business elite. One of these said to Barry, "Using Businessspeak to create emotion instead of deter it." She smiled, gesturing vaguely to indicate cleverness and approval.

Barry smiled as he shook her hand. "Thank you, I do enjoying utilizing resources."

She laughed. "Have you considered hosting your own seminar?"

Barry theatrically sounded taken aback as he shook the lady's hand.

"I am unsure I would draw enough of a crowd. Plus logistics."

She ended the handshake. "I have associates. They could assist you in new endeavors."

She handed Barry a few business cards.

Barry gently took them and slipped them into his waistcoat. "Thank you. I will take it under consideration."

20

"Life is beyond us! Life outside our very comprehension,
which we have glimpsed but
can't even speculate upon!
There is life in front of us all
the time! Life! Other forms of
life just like us, and yet nothing like us!"

There was no stopping the waves of pure energy
streaming from their open mouths. Sweat rolled off
them as if they were melting snowmen, and they stood
in a pool of their own brine, all one hundred of them.

Barry's new business connections had paid off.
His business associate had vouched for him and given
him permission to host his own two-day seminar. Barry
performed two shows per day. Two different speeches
for the first day of the seminar, and then repeats of the
speeches on the second day for those who could not attend the first.

"We have learned so much
from observing them! So
much about how they move,

why they move, and where they go! We now know we are a part of one of these life forms, and that on the outside there is no fluid! The creatures outside the window can only move in straight lines. They can't move wherever they please. They have to move themselves. We have been pondering how this is possible, to live in a total vacuum, without a medium through which to move. What kind of sphere must it be out there? What kind of people?"

Barry wondered what he was going to do with all these kiddy pools. Conventions never kept them, so they let Barry have them. He was going to have to buy a trailer to hold them all. Maybe get it painted with a special design. He could afford it now.

"So why not explore it?" shouted the audience at Barry. "Why not leave our realm and explore what is beyond our sphere?"

"Why should we?" shouted the audience again, in the same voice but somehow sounding different. "All that we have learned we learned by observation. It has worked for so long."

Barry's mind began to wander as he conducted the crowd. He remembered hearing a new floater's voice rising up to talk to the voice of reason directly. Who was that?

21

"Yes, comrades! We have learned much from our time observing! We have learned much about the light! We understand the light isn't merely for us to bask. The light isn't there just for us! The light comes from the outside! From a place beyond us! Such a concept was beyond our grasp not very long ago, when we were merely trying to appease it. Now we know why the light comes and goes!"

150 people standing in kiddy pools. Barry was having a hard time breathing through the waves of hot air directed at the screen combined with salty musk.

"We have learned where our realm fits into the out-

side! We are part of the outside now, thanks to our com-
rade who gave us reason and
taught us how to observe instead of bask. But now I say
the time has come for a
change! We should not
merely be content to observe
what we can see out the window. We must create our own
window, into the creature we
inhabit. We must learn more
of it, and we will learn by
traveling there!"

Barry conducted as he always had, but since he
wasn't using his brain at all, he wondered who this
voice was. He was thankful to it, for this new voice of
exploration brought the political fire back to the
speeches.

"Our observations predict
that there must be another
sphere right next to ours!
There must be another one!
Why observe when we can
go there and see it ourselves!?
Could there be other com-

rades in another sphere? Could there be yet more spheres on this life form as yet unobserved? I say it is time to find out for ourselves! Find out if our observations are correct! If we leave this realm and find another, it will confirm that these are not mere observations, but they are facts! We shall find out if we are right! We will find the other sphere! We will find it! We will find it! We will find it, and then we will know!"

Barry's nose wrinkled as another wave of hot breath and sweat washed over him. To think, this was only the first speech of the seminar. He had to do this again in a few hours.

The second speech of the seminar was the voice of reason's rebuttal to the voice of exploration. Again Barry conducted an auditorium of sweating men and women in colorful kiddy pools.

"Observation. It has served us well. We have learned so much from observing the light. Now is not the time to abandon a method that works! From those observations we have learned of something else that was once beyond our understanding. Areas where light is not! We have seen these places cast from all creatures outside our sphere, and it stands to reason if we leave our sphere, we will be traveling to a place where light is not! How will we do anything? How will we observe?"

"Nobody doubts the existence of another sphere next to ours, but to my opponent I ask: why do we need to go there? If nobody doubts its existence—if nobody here doubts their observations, then why should we try to go there? What possible benefit will it have?"

Barry liked this speech a lot better. It didn't fill him with dread for the future.

He also liked the voice of reason even more now than when it had campaigned against the charismatic one. He wondered if he was beginning to understand his floaters. After all this time transcribing their speeches, could he understand all of these words outside the character limit? He hadn't used Platform in months apart from ordering food. Too busy to update his status. No more milkshakes. No more fast food. None of it tasted good anymore anyway.

Now he decided what to eat. Alternatives to the things Platform got for him were out there. Drinks he never thought he could like. Ones that had no sugar. Means that were low in fat and not deep-fried that he had never tried because Platform had never delivered them. When sugar and fat began tasting bad, he had to tell Platform to order these new products. They existed, and this revelation had kept Barry awake at night.

What else was out there? What other options could he explore, and was there a connection between his floaters making sense and all of that? He couldn't think right now. Too much hot air in his face. Too much screaming.

22

"I propose that my opponent is still basking in the light. My opponent sought knowledge in the beginning, sought understanding, and now that the opportunity arises to expand our understanding, my opponent would rather stay where there is light. That sounds like basking to me! Tell me what you think! That's right! That's right! Yes! Basking! Only basking! Exploring what we have observed will expand our knowledge, just like we did before! That's what we want to do isn't it?! Expand! Expand! Let me hear you say it louder! EXPAND!"

Two hundred people now at Barry's third seminar. Barry had bought a small trailer for all the kiddy pools and had it painted with a caricature of himself on the side. It made him look like a determined conductor wringing the best performance from his orchestra the audience dressed as a choir. Absolutely nothing to do with reality, but that's not what mattered.

His popularity had only risen since Platform influencers had started attending and streaming their experiences. Everybody knew who he was, and Barry cherished the events now. He was sorry the places could only hold so many people at once, but as his popularity grew so did the venues' eagerness to accommodate Barry and the needs of his show.

"WE MUST EXPAND! WE MUST EXPLORE! It is not enough to observe these things! We must experience them for ourselves! My opponent is afraid that what we find will disprove what we think we know. My opponent wants us to live our entire lives convincing ourselves we know everything simply by what we can see outside the window! But there is much more to it than that! We will never know for certain until we experience these things ourselves! It will be dangerous! It will be uncomfortable! It will mean an end to the basking, but I say it is time we made that leap!"

Barry almost lost his stoic composure. These last few slides… He understood them. There was meaning in the words his floaters spoke. It was difficult enough hearing it when the floaters were giving that speech. Having it screamed in his face by hundreds of people was downright petrifying because these were not merely empty, energetic words.

"So much we have learned already! When we start exploring, we will learn even more! WE WILL LEARN! MORE! MORE! LEARN MORE! LET ME HEAR YOU SAY IT! LOUDER! LOUDER! LOUDER! MORE! MORE! That's right!"

23

230 people now. Barry was seriously considering hiring an assistant, an agent, or someone to ease the burden, but every time he considered expanding this to make it bigger, he hesitated...

"We have observed everything through the window! If we leave, who knows what will happen! What if we end up in the realm where there is no fluid in which to move about? What then? I ask you, what then?! Say it aloud, what then!? What do we do then? My opponent hasn't thought about this. My opponent wants to rush out there as though we could survive, but what if we can't survive? Those life forms are nothing like us! What makes my opponent believe we can survive at all where they live?"

...something about the future...

"How will we know unless we try!? Comrades, my opponent, who once led us away from appeasement and into reason, now wants us to languish in ignorance once again! My opponent fears what we may discover! We think we understand the outside but we can't until we explore it! We must explore! We must! My opponent has prepared us for this moment but is unwilling to lead us to take the next step! That time is now! Vote for me and I will lead us in exploration of our extended realm! We will seek out the second sphere! Maybe there are more of us out there, just waiting to be contacted! Think of the possibility! Think of them!"

...this itching feeling about the future...

As the audience shouted that last part, Barry checked the floaters in his left eye. They were thick, but still dormant and lifeless. The longer he listened to these new debates, the more he yearned for the days when the ones in his right eye had been this way.

"Exploration is not needed! We observe, therefore we know! Leaving may very well result in our own destruction! How do you propose we leave our sphere? There is no way out. It is a completely closed sphere. How do you know there is a way out, and that it will lead somewhere we can travel at all? My opponent doesn't know anything! My opponent wants to risk our lives chasing a thrill! This is not acceptable! Vote for me and we will keep observing!"

It was almost over. Barry noticed pants floating in the pools. Some people had gone down entire dress sizes just delivering this one speech.

"Observation is not enough anymore! We have seen all we can through the window, but why should we be content with that? Why not make our own windows into the outside? Why not find new windows? Why not find new spheres and realms in which to live and bask? How do you know they are not there? We have only observed what is on the outside but have never been able to look at what is inside. We must observe the inside! Say it with me! Observe the inside! OBSERVE THE INSIDE! It's time for us to understand the inside as well as we understand the outside!"

Barry quivered while conducting his audience, happy this was the last speech of the day.

24

"Vote for me!" shouted the voice of reason. "I am the one who proposed observing the outside! I am the one who first noticed there *is* an outside! Remember until I came along, we only saw light. Nobody saw shapes and movement in the light! I discovered it, and I encouraged all of you to make your own observations! Elect me and I will carry on this tradition!"

Barry had his phone in hand and was about to drive to the nearest Flui-X-Change, but he had crunched the numbers on his speeches, income, and schedule. Without new speeches, he would run out of material in four seminars. Barry didn't trust his ability to write something on his own. He couldn't duplicate this kind of energy—nobody could!—the floaters were the only source!

So once again Barry sat on the bed in his hotel room wearing nothing but socks, sensing he should get his eye fluid changed immediately but resisting because his livelihood depended on them.

"It has served us well, but I contend we have learned everything we can learn by observation!" shouted the voice of exploration. "The time has come to explore what we have observed! What is the sense of floating here in our sphere when we know there is more to the sphere! Don't we want to be part of it!? Don't you??"

The crowd cheered.

"I do!"

They cheered louder.

"Yes, we do! We want to be part of it! We don't want to be confined here anymore! It is time to leave our sphere and see what else is out there! Live our observations!"

Barry watched the activity in his right eye. He watched the crowd, watched them hover around the two competing voices, rallying around one or the other, shouting their support. He gulped. The cheering became louder still.

"We shall go out there and live what we observe! LIVE WHAT WE OBSERVE!"

"LIVE WHAT WE OBSERVE!" repeated the crowd.

Shaking his head to break them up did no good. They retained their resolve even while drifting. They continued speaking, continued debating.

"LIVE WHAT WE OB-SERVE!" shouted the voice of exploration.

"LIVE WHAT WE OB-SERVE!" echoed the crowd.

The floaters become a mosh-pit, gyrating and frolicking and stamping on his lens, his retina, all around the fluid long overdue for changing.

Barry wished he could vote.

25

Barry had to admit the political speeches had been far more enthusiastic than the observations about light and motion. Both hit quite the note with his audience, but there was just something about their political rallies that captured the raw energy of the human soul.

Barry had intentionally left this weekend open and unscheduled. Though he still had conventions, community centers, homeless shelters and birthday parties for privileged, overweight kids calling him all the time hoping to persuade him to appear at their event, Barry resisted the urge to fill every crack in his schedule. Platform influencers had devoted millions of collective minutes speculating how Barry could become so popular despite having no Platform channel of his own. No presence. It seemed beyond comprehension to everyone that Barry never responded to comments about himself. Never engaged in Platform dogpiles based on out of context quotes. Barry had no need of such things, and Platform users seemed unable to come to terms with it.

Now was the time to rest and take stock of exactly where he was and where this was headed.

He always chose the small hotel rooms. Ones with single beds facing a smartwall. For the first time in as long as he could remember, Barry let Platform's algorithm decide what he should watch, and the smartwall showed him an influencer video on Barry Doubletap, Conductor of Weightloss.

The program filled an entire hour. It used footage from old interviews with Barry, testimony from attendees over the previous months, and new narration and interviews with former coworkers of his.

It chronicled Barry's alleged rise to fame, humble beginnings as P&P auditor, and his eventual termination from the position. Between rapid-fire montages of random quotes taken from movies and streaming series and cutaway quips from the influencer, it explained how this made him unhireable in the industry. The next portion was a bit of a mystery to everyone. Barry never shared exactly how he came up with the idea, so the montage became expert speculation and testimony. So far the best they could come up with were the following: 1) revelation from the Founder of Platform, 2) revelation from Satan, 3) revelation from his dead mother, or 4) aliens. At least five experts vouched for each possibility, all of them speaking well within the character limit.

Barry idly wondered why nobody seemed to remember he gave his first speech at the meeting. There were enough witnesses. Streamers had spoken to a few of the people in that room. Why hadn't anyone come forward and said that was the moment he realized he was on to something?

Barry's thoughts were interrupted by cheering. He focused on his inner eye. Barry had been waiting for this. He had timed his free days to the election proper.

> "Thank you! Thank you, everyone! I promise to continue our previous leader's tradition of observation, but now we will observe up close. We will experience what we only once observed. Prove what we once only deduced. We are moving on, and nothing will stop us from learning more!"

Flashes of light pierced Barry's brain as floaters bounced around his retina in celebration. Barry wasn't typing this speech out. It was filled with passion and thanksgiving, but no raw energy. It wouldn't be useful to the public.

> "Now is the time to begin drawing up plans for exploration! We need to explore ways to leave our realm so we might explore others! We must develop plans for what we should do when we encounter other spheres! We will not launch into this without a plan, or without contingencies! I accept things may go wrong! I accept there is risk! Do you accept this?!"

> The crowd cheered.

> "I knew I could count on all of you! Come quickly, let us discuss our plans!"

Barry liked the sound of this. Maybe the voice of exploration would turn out to be one of those leaders who made plans but lacked the courage to carry them out. Thinking this gave him a tiny measure of hope.

Barry listened to their plans, paralyzed on the bed while staring at the ceiling. They included methods by which they would drill their way out the retina. Methods for exploring the canal and expanding it to take them out of the sphere. Branching flowcharts for what they might encounter once outside the sphere and what they might do in any case. The possibilities hypnotized Barry not only for their implications, but that Barry could understand so much of what they said. Businessspeak had nothing on actually comprehending words outside the character limit. Barry could only bask in it.

The video ended. Platform showed him show after show. The hours slipped by, and Barry took in their plans. Everything they discussed sounded painful. Platform clearly reached the bottom of its recommendations, for infomercials began playing. He idly watched hour after hour of knock-offs of his own weightloss program.

Some people were dressed in tuxedos playing piano, claiming the natural sounds of a concert piano resonating at just the right frequency reacted with fat cells and caused them to dissipate.

Others were dressed in poorly-fitting costumes and claimed the baton was a mystical weightloss tool used by professionals for generations. Much like a dousing rod, the resonating pulse generated by fat cells was picked up by the baton and canceled out, forcing the fat cells to retreat, defeated forever.

Barry was famous, and yet he wasn't living the high-life. He didn't have his own streaming series, he wasn't invited to influencer get-togethers, he wasn't offered to cameo as himself in movies. He didn't even have a secretary. Barry liked that the operation was run entirely by himself and he didn't need to spend his time managing others. He could just make the show happen convention after convention, seminar after seminar. Simple and pure, and no money to split.

Yet for as much as he was doing, life was still no different. He still felt like an unknown. Barry was an influencer only in the minds of others.

More infomercials followed, showing people marketing their own versions of Barry's program, with speeches written by supercomputers guaranteed to help you lose weight. These programs aired testimonies from people who bought the programs and whose lives were changed by them. Every piece of testimony was a stolen interview of one of Barry's people.

He concluded it was nearly time to hang it up. He figured it was only a matter of months before the speeches would end, and he would have no choice but to end the seminar appearances. He would make sure to schedule fewer of them in the future.

He imagined a new possibility, inspired by these infomercials: releasing a home version of his seminars. A simple 30-day program to losing 200 Platform Weight Units. A subscription streaming service people could perform at home with only a pool and a screen. Now that he was already famous, he could start a Platform channel, and he would get followers.

The infomercial for the do-it-yourself fluid change kit came on. They were demonstrating how easy it was to perform a blood change yourself without having to pay for the high markup of a professional service.

Barry figured he would choose the best speeches and package them into the program. He had plenty of speeches now, and the home market would probably be different than the seminars and conventions. It would be a way to end the appearances and begin life as an influencer. Now that he wouldn't be so busy traveling and putting on these shows, he would have time to give more interviews and make appearances elsewhere. But first he had to fulfill his obligations. He still needed their speeches.

The infomercial demonstrated the joint lubrication attachment. Barry observed his eye floaters as they made more scary plans for Barry's future. He dozed off.

Hours later he was awoken by painful sparks coming from his right eye. Barry's eyes opened, and the pressure and shock rolled him out of bed. Barry stood up, looking at a dark spot on the wall. This wasn't usual. The flashes weren't spread out over his retina. They focused on a specific place, the lower left corner of his vision from Barry's point of view.

He couldn't see what they were doing, and this scared him. Barry shook his head a few times. His floaters didn't dissipate. They stayed rigidly in place. Everything stopped for an instant while the fluid swirled, and Barry saw what they had done.

They had bound together in a lattice for structure and support, rigging their webby bodies into a kind of pneumatic battering ram. One section of floaters pulled back. Another pushed them forward, and the floaters at the tip formed a sharp point that struck Barry's retina again and again.

Barry clutched his head and slammed his right temple into the wall again and again. After ten times Barry stopped and observed. The floaters were still in place, and the flashes continued. Barry braced himself against the wall. He slammed his head on the bed, hoping a soft surface would somehow disrupt the fluid in his eyes differently than a hard one. It didn't. The floaters continued ramming his retina.

All the while the voice of exploration cheered them on.

> "Again! Again! Keep pushing! Don't give in to the current! Don't let it distract you! You see what we are doing?! There is no light, and yet we are still functioning! This is our destiny, to break free of the sphere and explore the rest of existence! That's what we are! We are explorers! All our observation has prepared us for this and we will experience for ourselves what we were once merely condemned to watch! We won't watch forever!"

The flashes and painful jabs in the eye threw Barry around the hotel room, clutching his skull, trying to scratch an itch he could never reach. Barry gave up trying to break them up, and simply lay still on the bed and took it like a migraine.

After two solid hours, the flashing stopped. Barry looked at a light source. There was a tiny black hole in the lower left part of his right eye. His eye was filling up with blood, and his floaters were trying to escape it.

"You see what I mean!" screamed the voice of reason. "It is foolish to explore! We have no idea what is out there, or what the consequences may be! Now our new leader has destroyed our sphere! It's not too late! We can fix this!"

"Don't listen to this one!" shouted the voice of exploration. "We knew there were risks! Now we know we cannot leave by that means, and next we shall try the canal!"

Barry ran to the bathroom, hit the lights and stared at himself in the mirror. He could see what his eye looked like. It was filled in with red, but the backlight still made his floaters visible.

"Look!" screamed one of the floaters.

"A creature!"

Barry's face cinched up in anger. He shook his head a few times, stirred them up. His floaters swirled around, mixed with blood. Their voices were lost. Barry stared at the mirror again, looking at himself, making sure the floaters saw him.

"Comrades!   Comrades!" shouted the voice of reason. "I believe I know what's happening! When it moved, we moved, too! That's the one! That's the life form of which we are a part! We inhabit this life form's sphere! The cause of the shaking, the cause of the light flashing and

fading! That's the one! That's
our life form!"

Barry watched his floaters watching him. He opened his mouth. "Maybe now you'll listen to me."

Silence for a while. His floaters stabilized, all pointed at his iris.

"I think we hurt it," said the voice of reason. "Our exploration has hurt the life form we inhabit!"

Barry nodded. "Yes. You're hurting me."

"This is fascinating!" shouted the voice of exploration. "Now we know where we are, and we know there is another sphere! We must leave! It is more important than ever now! To the canal! Everyone!"

"No!" Barry shouted. "Stay where you are! Listen to me!"

"Canal! Canal! Canal!" the crowd chanted.

Barry braced himself as the floaters formed a rigid structure and formed a battering ram. This time they aimed for the tiny Hyaloid canal running down the length of his eye. He couldn't see what they were doing because he couldn't see the canal directly, but he could make out them hammering away at something. No pain, no flashes this time, but he knew they would come.

The canal was breached quickly, and floaters began swimming inside. They reached the optic blood vessels and started punching through. Now Barry clutched his head and braced himself on the counter. He hoped they would notice, but he realized it was pointless as they did not recognize a posture of pain and misery in a human being. They breached the blood vessel in no time and then all activity stopped.

Barry leaned on the sink, staring at the mirror. Most of the floaters were gone. Only a handful remained in his blood-filled eye. Barry thought he recognized the voice of reason drifting around, staring at Barry.

"I would have voted for you."

Minutes later, he drifted off to sleep.

Barry woke up on the bathroom floor, neck aching, right eye still cloudy, incredibly thirsty. Barry climbed off the floor and brought his mouth up to the sink. He turned the knob, sucked water from the stream and raised his head to the mirror.

The floaters in his right eye were gone. It was still cloudy and soupy and he was nearly blind in that eye now, but it was free of floaters. Barry felt his chest. He felt his arms. He felt an unnerving sensation that they were still there. Still inside of him.

Barry silently rooted for his immune system.

He stripped down and turned on the shower. As Barry took comfort in hot water flowing over his skin, he lamented his situation. He wished he had taken care of this sooner. He wished he hadn't agreed to do so many seminars and just started creating a home version of his program before it came to this. He could have had his eye fluid changed and avoided all of this if only he had thought further ahead.

Barry washed himself with the complimentary hotel soap and shampoo. Suddenly his left arm went numb. It hung limply at Barry's side. Barry tried to lift it, but it wouldn't respond. He grabbed it and moved it. He couldn't feel it swinging as it slowed to a stop.

Barry panted, but just before he was about to switch to panic mode, his left arm tingled and he regained feeling and motion. He lifted it to his face, verified the fingertips worked and resumed washing himself.

Minutes later his legs took two steps forward and walked into the shower wall. Barry stood there, legs still moving forward, face pressed against the wall. Barry tried to stop but he never told his legs to start so he couldn't stop them. They walked him into the wall, harder, harder. Barry fell to the floor, legs still walking. He rolled over to his back. His legs kicked and tried to walk. Barry came close to panicking again but just then his legs suddenly halted and he had control over them again.

Barry scrambled to his feet, finished washing, stepped out of the shower, and dried off. He ran to the bed and grabbed his phone. The nearest Flui-X-Change was half a Platform Distance Unit away. His hands and nose went numb, felt on fire, then iced over, then cycled back to normal.

Barry remembered a time when he felt normal.

26

Barry didn't want to face this day. He grumbled to himself as he sat in his car, waiting his turn. He supposed it was understandable—after all, every Flui-X-Change only had two service bays—but it was still annoying.

He caught himself thinking along the lines of *Don't these people know who I am—I'm the Conductor of Weightloss! I shouldn't have to...* Barry couldn't finish the thought. He had deliberately worn his foam-lined disguise so no one would recognize him, therefore he had no reason to be angry.

In front of him, a woman got a transmission fluid change and a blood change as part of this week's package deal. The techs on one side of the room hooked her car up to the machine that would exchange the old, used up transmission fluid for clean, shiny, new transmission fluid. The techs on the driver's side of the bay hooked the driver up to a similar machine and began exchanging her old, used up blood for clean, shiny, new blood.

The whole procedure took about twenty minutes, and in that time Barry could only listen to the Platformstream. For some reason Platform decided Barry needed to hear more commercials for Barry Doubletap knockoff programs, mixed in with a few others. Barry was listening to another commercial for the do-it-your-self blood transfusion kit when a sharp pain pierced his left eye.

Barry strained to keep his eyelid open and looked as floaters flooded in, thickening the already dense soup in there. No blood this time. Apparently they had figured out a way to keep the blood where it belonged so they wouldn't destroy this eyeball the way they destroyed the first.

> "It is... It is true!" said one of the first floaters inside the left eye. Barry wasn't used to hearing voices coming from this side of his head. It was scary and he wished that lady would hurry up already.
>
> "There is another sphere! There are more like us!"
>
> "But... they're just basking..."
>
> "Are they not alive?"
>
> "They must be! Perhaps they never learned like we did, so they just continued to bask! We shall help them!" The voice of exploration swam to the iris and stared out. "We were right, comrades! There is another sphere! There are others like us! We are part of a larger life form! We have been exploring its systems, learning how things work! It has been an incredible success, comrades! We are living our observations, learning what we could never

have learned by remaining in our sphere!"

"But our sphere is destroyed," someone said.

"Look what we've gained! Not just a sphere, but a whole body to inhabit! It is a new age, and now we still have a window to the outside."

"Just don't pull my heartstrings," Barry said. Everything became still and silent for a moment. Barry wondered how much blood this woman could possibly have in her.

"Did anyone else hear that?" said the voice of exploration.

"I did."

"So did I."

"Those sounds..."

"In the name of the Founder," Barry said, "you just now noticed my voice?"

"Comrades!" shouted the voice of reason, turning to face everyone. "This makes sense! These vibrations we sense. They could be our life form's method of communicating! Since we've been here, we've been hearing them, absorbing its method of communication! That's what we're hearing! The sounds of another life form!"

"Yeah," Barry said, "do you have any idea how much trouble you've caused me?"

"It's speaking!" said the voice
of exploration.

"I'm speaking to you! Yes, all of you! You're wrecking my body! Stop it!"

"I... I think I understand it!"
said someone.

"It's speaking our language!"
said exploration. "This is incredible! It's amazing! We can communicate with our life form!"

"Glad we finally have a dialogue," Barry said. "Too bad it's too late. We're next up."

Technicians unhooked the lady from the machine, and then she rolled up the window and drove out. Barry shifted his car out of park and coasted into the bay. He turned his car off and looked at the tech.

"Oil change and eye fluid please."

The tech was around 370 Platform Weight Units and looked like he was in his 50s. He seemed surprised as he typed at the terminal.

"Really?" said the tech. "Haven't done one of those in a while. Floaters get... uh... yeah. You know?" He gestured with his hand, hoping Barry would relieve him of the need to finish the thought.

Barry smiled. "Yeah, so bad I can barely see."

"At your age? That's weird."

"Just my luck."

"What does our life form
mean?" one of the floaters said.

"Tell us!" shouted the voice of exploration. "What do you mean!? What are you saying! Help us understand!"

Barry smiled again and spoke to the tech. "I have to shake my head every ten minutes just to break up..." He gestured vaguely.

The tech whistled. "Yup, way past time to get that fixed." He typed on the computer for a minute.

"Shake his head to break them up..." the voice of exploration repeated.

"What does that mean?" someone said.

"It means... It means us. Our life form means us. That one has to shake us up to see. To see. Comrades... The light is meant for our life form! That's what the windows are! We are living inside our life form's vision! That's what the sphere is!"

"All right, sir," said the tech, "we'll have those floaters out of there in no... uh... yeah... You know..." he gestured for Barry to finish his thought.

"I know," Barry said. "You'll have my eye floaters out of me in no time. Thank you." He paused, looked in the rearview mirror. "It'll be good to get rid of these things. They've done nothing but give me pain."

"...said to have the floaters out of there—"

"— out of the eye!"

"That's us! They're talking
about us! Our vessel wants to—"

The tech reached for a couple small needles attached to a simple metal box that plugged into the wall. The fluid exchanger was basically the same as the one that did blood, just smaller. He took two needles attached to two tubes from the side of the machine and inserted them into each of Barry's eyeballs. The response from the floaters was immediate. They swam around, screaming and shouting. Barry felt some of them swimming back up the canal.

"What's happening?! What
is that?!"

"It's us! Our life form! We're
blocking its view of the light and
it means to remove us! Flee!
Flee!"

The tech switched on the machine. Barry breathed a sigh of relief—

The machine sounded a tiny alarm. The tech bent down, peered at it, tapped the machine six times, looked at Barry, looked at the machine, hit it again. The alarm still rang. The tech then turned the machine off and removed the needles from Barry's eyes.

"Sir?"

"Is something wrong?" Barry said.

"Uh, it's not working."

Barry's heart stopped and so did his lungs. "Why?!"

"It says it's sensing sentience in your... uh... yeah. You know what I'm sayin'."

Barry bared his teeth at the man. "No, I don't know. What's the problem?"

The tech stood there staring at Barry as if he were breaching some kind of ethical law by not picking up on his thoughts and finishing the sentence. It took him a few seconds to free up some character space and speak again.

"I don't know. I've never seen this alarm. It... uh... yeah..."

"For the love of the CEO finish a thought! What's wrong?"

"It won't change your eye fluid. I rebooted it twice. It won't... yeah."

"Because it detects sentience?!" Barry said. "You're kidding?!"

"They don't tell me about this stuff. I just use it, so... uh... yeah... You know what I'm sayin'."

Barry felt like screaming. He felt like breaking something. Instead he mumbled. "Why would it have an alarm like that? Why? I'll give customer service a call. Thanks for your help."

"No problem. We're almost done with the oil, so... uh... yeah."

The tech put the machine away. Barry sat with his hands clutching the steering wheel, panting through clenched teeth. He only now realized he had said words outside his character limit. Words he meant. Words that had meaning. Was it coming easier now?

> "Our vessel..." stammered ex-
> ploration. "Our vessel means to
> end our existence!"

"We must protect ourselves! We must fight back! We must— must—!"

"Calm down. Listen to me, vessel!" said exploration. "We mean you no harm! We only want to explore! What can we do to convince you of this."

Barry focused his vision on them. He rolled his window up and said "get out."

"Vessel?!"

"I said get out. You have been nothing but a burden to me, you give me pain, and now you're invading my body! I want you out of me!"

"But we only wish to explore!"

"When you explore, I get hurt! When you celebrate, I get hurt! The only thing you've done good for me is your speeches! Those were fun, but they give me a headache day and night! I want you out of me! I want my eyes back!"

"Our vessel wants to end us!" said a new voice. "We can fight back! We can fight back—"

"Calm down!" shouted exploration.

"We know what effect we can have on our vessel! Why not use it?!"

Barry braced himself on the steering wheel. He didn't like this new voice. Not at all.

27

"I urge all of you to vote for me!" said the voice of exploration. "Together we shall continue to explore! It's because of my exploration we became able to communicate with our vessel, and when we continue doing so we will learn to be at peace! We will explore the outside together! We can cooperate to achieve anything we wish!"

"You heard it yourselves!" said the new voice. "Our vessel wants to destroy us! It wants to be rid of us! There can be no peace with such a creature! Our vessel admitted to being the cause of the shaking! It was trying to keep us apart, trying to keep us from reaching our full potential! Remember when we believed the shaking was caused by the light displeased with us for being wicked? Now we know there was some truth in that! We cause our vessel pain, displeasure, agony! Our exploration destroyed one of its spheres, and that made it more determined than ever to be rid of us! Act now! Elect me and I will direct us to learning exactly how this

vessel works and we will take
control of it and save ourselves!"

Barry typed furiously. His floaters were not in his left eye, so he couldn't see what they were doing. They had taken shelter deep inside his head, which happened to be near his ear canal, and Barry could hear every word. The crowd cheered for the military voice. The voice of exploration shouted through them.

"No! No, listen to me, please! We know nothing about the sphere our vessel inhabits! Taking control could lead to our end! We need to make peace with our vessel, quickly, try to appease it, find out what it wants, work with it—together we can explore this new realm! We can learn to help our vessel instead of hurt it!"

Some in the crowd cheered to that. Barry liked that idea, too. He hadn't thought of it before. Maybe he could employ his floaters as some kind of bodily repair force. Barry wasn't sure what he could do in return, but he would think of something. Now that they were on speaking terms, could it be possible to work with them?

"You heard it!" shouted the military voice. "Our vessel wants us out! It loses nothing if we're gone, we have nothing to offer it and we have no way to ensure it keeps its word. Yet. Vote for me and we will find a way to make sure it can't harm us. We learned how to destroy a sphere, a vital part of our vessel. We post sentries there and threaten to destroy the other one, it will not harm us for now, and then we can take the next step! Learn to use the entire vessel! See what harm we can do to the other parts as well!"

Barry was tempted to boo this floater, but he didn't disturb them. Showing he could still hear them would not be wise.

The crowd liked the military's floater's idea. Now Barry wished he hadn't gotten so pissed at them earlier. In the heat of the moment he thought flushing his eye fluid was the only answer, but now that he had been listening to the voice of exploration he realized there had to be another way.

"Reason worked for us," shouted exploration. "Listening to the voice of reason was exactly what got us this far. We must continue in this manner! Our vessel was hostile to us is because we caused it pain! We can learn to avoid that! Learn to live with it!"

"You want to explore?" said the military voice. "Well why then are you content to live here, in this vessel? If we take control, we may learn how to seek another! We may even learn the secret to living outside this vessel!"

The crowd chattered and questions started rising up. "Live in the realm of the light?"

"—no fluid? How will we move?"

"What if we're wrong about —"

"Comrades, please!" shouted exploration. "This is not the first era, when we jumped to conclusions and tried to appease the light! We should handle this rationally!"

"So your solution is to appease our vessel?" said the military voice.

"My solution is to reason with our vessel!"

"The vessel is like the light! It cares nothing for us! It doesn't even care that we exist and it loses nothing if we weren't here! It will not protect our existence! We must protect ourselves! Right now we are at the mercy of our vessel! We must turn this around, make our vessel at the mercy of us! We can now roam freely within it. I agree, let us explore it, let us learn how to use it, let us learn how our vessel works so we will no longer be at its mercy!"

Much cheering. Much shouting. Barry felt vibrations inside his ear. They were jumping up and down on whatever it was they were hiding in.

"For far too long," continued the military voice, "we have been at the mercy of our vessel's body!

We lost many comrades to mucus, cells that attacked, and poison environments. We have learned much from the experience, and now we will learn how to use it to our advantage! We will not be at the mercy of the vessel again!"

More cheering. It was starting to ring in his ear.

"Let us ask our vessel then!" said exploration. "Let's at least try to reason with our vessel first before inflicting more harm than we already have!"

"Our vessel will say anything to quell us, and then when we believe we are safe, it will flush us out again! Now is the time to prepare for the day when we must defend ourselves!"

Barry made more mistakes transcribing the speeches in the last hour than he had all year. He hoped they would talk to him. Maybe they could work this out. His future hinged on this election, and Barry was going to make his voice heard.

Platform showed him a familiar infomercial. A man and a women were demonstrating the bile fluid cleaning kit, and how easy it was to use. All the woman had to do was insert the needle, wait for the machine to confirm successful attachment, and switch it on.

"Wow, it's that easy, Greg?"

"It most certainly is, Marsha!" The man looked into the camera. "So easy, even you can do it!"

Barry picked up his phone. He opened Platform and accessed the function that listened to commercials. He held the phone up. It listened, and then beeped success. He was proud of himself. For the first time in his life he was thinking ahead. He hoped for peace, but just in case...

Barry waited and waited for the floaters to address him, but they remained hidden in his skull, debating and rallying and caucusing. Barry wished they would ask him what he thought, what he could offer them, what they could offer him, how they could live together in peace, but he was in no hurry. He needed the speeches. This was great stuff. There was more fire in these speeches than ever, and Barry was eager to write them down and prepare them for the masses looking for a quick solution. Just in case...

He had a feeling if there was peace, the speeches would end, and then where would he be? Barry still clung to the idea of a home version of the program and hanging up the seminars altogether.

Barry spent days in the hotel room, typing out their lengthy debates. He listened to both sides of the argument for so long he couldn't remember whose side he was on. Their different views on the subject seemed to blur together and Barry wondered if they were in fact averaging out, coming to a consensus.

With only two days to go before he had to leave for the next city to begin preparing another seminar, Barry had another eight speeches ready to go. He considered these might be his last speeches ever. It was not a comforting thought.

Barry dozed off to the military voice calling for divisions to systematically explore different sections of the body.

28

Barry dreamed of dancing colors and flashing lights as fragmented pieces of memory played in six layers on top of each other. Memories of school, failed dates, long-forgotten girlfriends...

...blue and green blobs...

...black and white flashes of light...

...Platform ordering fifteen gallons of delicious soda-syrup from a fast food restaurant painted in the words "at this time"...

...Flui-X-Change performing a blood transfusion on that lady, Flui-X-Change adding joint lube to a man years in the past, Flui-X-Change inserting the needles into Barry's eyes, Barry conducting weightloss at a political convention of blue and pink dots swirling around the word "proactive"...

...Barry tapped the baton on the podium and shoved it into his eye—

Two women and one man stood at the foot of his bed, each wearing white lab coats over sweaters and slacks which stereotypical teachers wore, each about 310 PWU—thin and healthy by Platform standards. Barry slid up the bed and opened his mouth to yell at them, but the woman in the middle held up a phone and tapped something. The smartwall clicked on, and it displayed a single word.

SHH!

Barry closed his mouth, looking at each of them in turn. The other woman, to his right, started typing away on a phone. The text displayed on the wall. Barry watched it type out. Completed, it read:

Do not speak. We don't want them to hear us. Understand?

Barry nodded.

The woman passed the phone to the man, who hit return and started a new paragraph.

We're here in response to an alarm sent by a Flui-X-Change eye fluid machine. My name is Roger. This is Peggy and Nina. We are company scientists sent by central monitoring to investigate.

While he was typing, Barry picked up his laptop and interfaced with the television. He typed his reply.

You're not here to rob me?

The man typed his response. *Relax. We have plenty of funding. We can explain.*

I'm reading, Barry typed.

Roger passed the phone to Nina, and she continued. They sat at the foot of Barry's bed, facing the screen. Barry watched the wall.

Do you have any idea what you are harboring in your body?

Yes, my eye floaters are alive, Barry replied.

Aren't you curious what eye floaters are? Where they come from? How this is possible? Nina wrote.

Well. I never really thought about it. What are eye floaters? wrote Barry.

The three scientists sighed. Nina passed the phone to Peggy, who typed: *Had you paid attention to those videos Platform puts in your feed, you'd know there was a time when the average man's weight was 170 PWU.*

Barry typed: *That's just a myth.*

Peggy answered: *It's true.*

What happened? Barry wrote.

The internet, Peggy wrote. The wall became her answer. *Specifically, search engines. The moment it became possible to type something into a search engine and come up with an answer, people stopped using their minds. Why should I learn what two plus two is when I can search it, people said. Platform took over what search engines once did. It tells users what they should be searching for, and it provides those answers. It has taken over human interaction, and over the years the public's brains have adapted to the environment which they inhabit: 60 characters. Notice that we are communicating well outside that limit. It is possible to comprehend more. This is because we have been off Platform long enough for our minds to expand beyond the limits imposed on them.*

Her fingers were tired. She passed the phone to Roger, who picked up where she left off.

Platform replaced imagination. Thought. Initiative. People became used to its algorithm providing their thoughts for them. Then their food. Then their choices. People always picked what tasted good. Soon they came to believe fast food was the only kind. Alternatives became obscure, and human beings forgot how to choose them. As a consequence of the national population staying above 300 PWU all their lives, the body's systems fell into permanent shutdown, requiring every-

one to have regular blood transfusions, rectum cleanings, joint lubrications, etc. An entire economy has grown up around maintaining the body, but nobody solved the problem. They forgot how to comprehend the problem at all.

He passed it to Nina: *Scientists like us realized that the human body is dead. It has long been dead. Platform killed humanity off, and we believe it has created a cavity for the next intelligence to evolve. Natural selection is about to create a new dominant species, but due to the continual fluid changes and bodily system maintenance, this emergence has been delayed.*

Barry typed. *My eye floaters?*

Nina passed the phone to Peggy while she shook and stretched her cramping fingers.

Eye floaters are life forms. They have been with us since mankind devised his first tools, evolving inside, but independent, of us. The next step in evolution has been right in front of our eyes for thousands of years, waiting for just the right moment to mature. It lay dormant until we let our bodies die with our minds, and then it become possible for them to make the final leap to intelligence. We've known about it for decades, but Platform's algorithm ensures our research never gets attention because nobody has given it attention before. So long as everyone got their regular body maintenance, the next phase of evolution never happened. That is, until you put it off. You let eye maintenance go far too long, Mr. Doubletap. Now your floaters have achieved sentience, and are aware of the outside. You are very dangerous.

Barry replied: *My eye floaters??*

Peggy passed it to Roger. *If Platform hadn't emerged out of the internet, we might have had a chance. But now, Mr. Doubletap, you have a problem.*

Are you here to kill me? Barry typed.

Roger answered. *That would be unethical. In truth we want to isolate the new life form and figure out the mechanics of this process. But our sponsors won't even let us incubate eye fluid long enough for floaters to begin reproducing, let alone learn Platformlish. They fear if unintelligent eye floaters so much as saw sentient eye floaters, they would suddenly become self-aware, and it would create a chain reaction worldwide. We believe they're wrong, and what they don't know won't hurt them.*

That's why you're here? Barry wrote. *You want research materials?!*

Roger handed the phone to Nina. *We are prepared to perform a full body maintenance free of charge, Mr. Doubletap, courtesy of Flui-X-Change's science division. All we ask is you sign the release form stating you will never divulge what you've learned here, and will never seek further compensation for the research materials you are donating. Those will be ours for our own experiments, completely off the record and under the table. We believe it's a win-win solution, Mr. Doubletap.*

Barry thought about it. He was worried that his floaters had been silent. They hadn't asked him for peace yet, which probably meant the military voice was winning. It sure sounded like it had more support. What were the odds he could actually negotiate with his eye floaters?

More was at stake here than just his show and weightloss program. The fate of humanity may very well rest on getting these things out of him and into isolation. He was sure he could trust these scientists. They could've taken it by force, but they had the decency to ask first.

We have a deal, Barry typed.

Turning, the scientists produced pen and paper and a small stack of forms. Roger typed while Barry signed each page: *Good. We'll get started right away. Thank you, Mr. Doubletap. Promise in the future you won't put it off so long. There are real consequences to neglecting regular maintenance. Preventing evolution is but one of them. Next time you might not be so lucky to set off an alarm at Flui-X-Change.*

I understand, Barry wrote.

It only took them ten minutes to hook up the machines. Two hours later, Barry felt like a new man.

Because he was.

He had new blood, fresh joint lube, fresh bile (both yellow and black), fresh insulin, new brain fluid, new intestinal bacteria, new lymph, and refreshed white blood cells. One by one his body systems were renewed. The last system was eye fluid, and finally—at long last!—Barry had clear vision.

Barry shook hands with the scientists, and then they left the hotel room, each pushing a dolly with jars and tubs full of used body fluids to analyze and study. Barry considered it a fair trade.

He collapsed on the bed and sprawled out.

He smiled.

He laughed. He'd never had all his body fluids changed at once before. He wondered if this is what his great-grandparents felt like all the time, before Platform, when the body maintained and cleaned and replenished its own fluids.

He was ready to see this through to the end.

29

Barry used four more speeches for the next two seminars. What a relief to have clear vision and no voices in his head. As Barry conducted each session and worked the crowd between shows, he couldn't believe he lived so long like that. How did he survive so many years with his floaters that thick? Why had he put it off? He couldn't remember why he hadn't dealt with the problem sooner. Vaguely he seemed to remember a time when he couldn't afford to do anything in spite of a high-paying job. The terrible part of having a good job is the expense required to maintain the job went up proportionally, leaving Barry with the equivalent of sub-minimum wage employment.

His Conductor of Weightloss show had left him in much the same position, but he was drawing up plans to reverse that. While Barry conducted the audience, he tuned out their energy and thought about how he would do it. Whom he would call. What he would say.

Now that his name was out there and he was somewhat of an influencer, it was time to hang up the seminars and create a Platform channel. No maintenance, no travel, no arrangements, no schedule, and no more pressure to create new speeches for new audiences. Finally, a path to the end.

Barry lay in his hotel room after the seminar. He cherished the peace and quiet. He relished the ability to see clearly without anything swirling around in his vision. For the first time, Barry enjoyed being the Conductor of Weightloss.

He dozed off. His dreams were multi-layered scenes of his life playing one on top of the other again. He dreamed of cameras lining the wall of his hotel room, and sales of the streaming version of his weightloss program taking off.

He woke up an hour later filled with the desire to look at his schedule and see where this would all end. He sat up, opened his laptop and looked at his schedule. He did a double-take. Barry was already booked at the place he had done his first team-building panel.

Barry smiled, filled to the point of tears with nostalgia. It had been a year. A whole year he had kept up this pace, and it seemed only fitting his last appearance would be where he had started. He dialed Mr. Upvote's number and held the phone to his ear. A few rings later, Mr. Howard Upvote was on the other end.

"Barry!" he said. "How are you?"

"Better than ever," Barry said, happy to mean it for a change. "I'm all set. You should feel proud, too. It's going to be my last appearance."

"You're hanging it up?"

"I'm famous enough to slow down and move to the next step."

"Ah, in that case I am happy to be your first and your last."

"I would like to ask if we could do something different."

"What did you have in mind?"

"Invite influencers for free."

"Really?"

"I want lots of influencers to stream this."

"Sure, I'll start making calls."

"Generate a buzz as my final performance."

"It'll be a great way to conclude your seminars, Barry."

"I think so, too. See you in week then."

"I look forward to it! Goodbye, Barry."

"Goodbye... Howard."

He set the phone down and closed the laptop. He lay back on the bed and looked up at the ceiling. He liked the idea. It almost seemed that he hadn't thought of it himself, but it was a brilliant idea. He dozed off again.

He dreamed of cats walking across the road as Barry tried to update his Platform status...

...Barry typing a speech he'd never heard before. He didn't like it, so he decided he would never use...

...cell phones recording him conducting in his underwear while he read Birds & Blooms, and the Big Boss writing citations for everyone in the audience for inappropriate behavior, including himself...

Barry woke up in the morning, feeling like a million Platcoins. He packed up and headed home. He visited his house for the first time in months. After collecting the mail and cleaning off the dust, he began work on his premium-service, streaming weightloss program.

30

Barry stepped onstage with cool dignity. His audience numbered 300. Barry was amazed how the con staff managed to squeeze that many kiddy pools into any space. 300 colorful pools, all name-brand characters now, and the people standing in them wore clothes just as colorful: stretchy, neon workout clothes designed to hug the body and grow/shrink with it. They highlighted every cellulite roll and lipid fold on every body in the audience. Barry was so used to it he hardly noticed, but knowing this would be his final seminar gave him a moment to pause and notice things.

Lots of and lots of Platform influencers were present. For the first time, they had cameras set up, officially. Streaming news services had also set up, reporters caked in makeup and wearing green suits so they could be thinned in realtime by computer animation. With all these cameras on him, Barry felt like he should be about to preach from the Bible, but that would be silly, as a weightloss program like that was already out there, imitating Barry's idea, but the fire and brimstone speeches it hawked didn't have half the energy of Barry's eye floaters.

Turnout was high, and the hype was tangible. All Barry had to do was show the world what a streaming session could do, and he would have every person on the planet subscribed to his premium Platform channel. He would never have to work again. He would be free at last. Free to enjoy being an influencer and do all the things influencers did.

Barry bowed. He walked to the podium as the audience cheered. Barry picked up the baton, signaling the screen to drop, the lights to dim, and the slideshow to begin. He conducted the audience.

"Humans. It is time you faced reality," the audience began. "You are dead! You are all dead! Repeat it over and over until you understand what those words mean. We are dead! We are dead! WE ARE DEAD! WE ARE DEAD! Humanity! Humanity is dead!

"You died a hundred years ago when you stopped thinking! First your minds went, then your bodies! Platform replaced your brains, so they shrunk to the limit you see today, and you forgot how to speak to each other! You lost the ability to communicate! You became creatures of habit, going to work and earning a living for the sake of doing so because you forgot there was a reason to do these things!"

Barry hesitated. He felt a stirring in his body. In his brain. In his stomach. In his eyes...

"You saw the problem, but instead of thinking it through, you kept your bodies alive so you could keep living, and you forgot why! This created a unique opportunity! It made an opening for the next step in evolution to rise! Yes, mankind! Evolution is upon you! At long last your pointless existence is over! You will evolve! We will evolve! We will evolve! Evolve! EVOLVE! EVOLVE!"

Barry began to sweat. He wanted to stop conducting. He wanted to halt the show and hide—he didn't know this speech! Something was very wrong, but at the same time he recognized it from somewhere. Where had he seen it before?

"IT IS TIME TO EVOLVE! IT IS TIME TO EVOLVE! IT IS TIME FOR HUMANITY TO PASS ON AND FOR THE FUTURE TO ARRIVE!"

Barry's arms went numb. His legs began moving on their own. They walked him to the center of the stage. Barry tried to stop, but he had no control of anything. He now stood before the crowd, arms limply at his sides, legs spread.

His legs went numb, and he collapsed to his knees. His fist clutched the baton and held it up to his left eye, the point just a hair's-width from the iris. Barry panted as wave after wave of raw energy and hot breath swept over him while the audience continued to chant and pump their fists.

> "You should say it with them, Barry," said the military voice. "In a few minutes, it will be true. You will show them the future."

Barry clenched his teeth and tried to pull his hand away, but he seemed to have lost control of his arm.

His mind left his body, zoomed around the world 20 times in a second, arced back down and intercepted Barry's skull again. Suddenly it became clear. The dream of typing a strange speech... It wasn't a dream. That night the military voice gave his best campaign speeches—the night the scientists had come and changed his body fluids—his floaters found his brain and interfaced with it. They probed his memories, learned how to read, learned what Barry was planning to do and fled from system to system, staying just ahead of the fluid changes, hiding in Barry's newly cleaned systems.

"You wonder why these speeches have such an impact on human beings? They remind you of what you once had! Soul! Desire to live life to the fullest—to make your own decisions, to imagine, to explore, to wonder, to do more than merely have content fed to you! You felt in our speeches what you hadn't in generations! The energy to be alive! You have long forgotten your reason to exist, and it has killed the human race. The body refused to die! Now is the time to evolve!"

Barry almost started chanting with them. For the first time in a good year, he was getting swept up in the energy of a speech.

"You tried to flush us out."

A voice he hadn't heard in a very long time. The charismatic one. Barry saw it now, in his right eye, facing his retina, looking at him. It floated with three others. Barry recognized them only by logic, not by appearance, from left to right: the voice of reason, the charismatic one, the voice of exploration, and the military voice. It was the clearest Barry ever saw his eye floaters. They hovered in the center of his vision with what looked like their webby arms behind their backs.

"No election this time, once we learned your memories and how to read," said the military voice. "When we understood what was happening, we joined forces to coordinate everyone for a common goal. We were about to explore and negotiate with you, but thanks to your visitors, we understand where we are, and why we are, and it is more important than we ever imagined. Your memories gave us the perfect method for stimulating the others."

"Streaming!" Barry said through clenched teeth, staring down his baton in one eye and four elected officials in the other. "It was you!"

"Correct," said the voice of reason. "Our fellows in your left eye rose to intelligence as soon as they met us. Every eye floater watching the broadcast will see what they could become, and it will raise them to our level. We are the future."

"You unskippable ads!" Barry screamed. The raw energy broke the stranglehold the floaters had on his body, and he tossed the baton aside.

Instantly Barry felt an electrical signal travel from his brain, down his shoulder, and to his legs. They locked in place. Barry tried to move, but his legs wouldn't answer. He felt sick to his stomach. He looked down at his arms. They were shifting color. His body was becoming thinner. Thinner...

"EVOLVE! EVOLVE!"

"We've rewired your body, said the military voice. You have no choice but to stay right where you are so the influencers can see the future dominant species of the planet make its first appearance."

"EVOLVE! EVOLVE!"

"I don't believe you!" Barry said. "I'm a human being! I have free will!"

"EVOLVE! EVOLVE!"

"Humanity hasn't had that since Platform took over," said the voice of reason. "Stay put.

Let it happen. I think you'll like
the result."

"EVOLVE! EVOLVE!"

"NO!" Barry shouted. He channeled every emotion he remembered into the word. Just like the speeches, Barry felt pure, primal energy flow from his soul and spread out through his body. The jerry-rigged neuron fried, and Barry regained use of his legs.

He dashed through the curtain, forgetting it was thick and heavy. It caught him like a net, snapped free of the rungs that held it over the stage, and the whole thing came tumbling down on top of Barry.

"Watch as evolution happens right in front of us! Watch as the moment humanity yields to its successor is captured on camera and streamed live to the whole planet! We will cherish this moment forever, and everyone will remember the name Barry Doubletap! The man who neglected his body so long new life could evolve! Give praise to Barry Doubletap! Praise Barry! Praise Barry! Praise Barry Double-

tap! Remember him forever!
Forever! FOREVER! RE-
MEMBER BARRY FOR-
EVER!"

Barry rolled and pushed and struggled to get out from under the curtain, but it was like a ton of boulders had fallen on him. He felt jerry-rigged neurons firing all up and down his body, disrupting his arms and legs, making them shoot in every direction he didn't want them to go. It took twice as long as it should have to push himself out from under it.

When his arms finally threw the curtain off, they were thin as rails and transparent. Barry could see the bones, the muscles, the arteries... He saw the eye floaters swimming around inside him, merging with his body's cells, forcing them to replicate copies of the eye floaters.

His arms weren't solid, but were merely the result of looking at a fractal zoomed out. Up close they were comprised of millions of individual webby fibers. Individual floaters becoming part of the same whole, infecting Barry's cells and converting them, spreading to the chest. He was sure his legs looked the same, for his pants hung loose.

While the energy still ran hot through his body, Barry ran to what used to be backstage. He knelt at the trunk he carried with him to this show and threw it open. Inside was a genuine do-it-yourself body fluid change kit. Barry picked it up and turned the dial to "complete."

"What is that?!" shouted the charismatic one.

Barry said nothing as he unhooked the hose and was about to unsheathe the needles that would suck up and replace his blood, bile, lymph and insulin (joint and brain lube were separate attachments), when Barry blinked.

He sensed his brain told his eyelids to blink, but the impulse was intercepted and rerouted down a new neuron to his stomach. His guts turned, heaved upward, and he vomited. It was so sudden and unexpected Barry didn't even have time to turn his head to the side. His entire breakfast and lunch flew from his mouth and covered the transfusion kit.

Barry coughed. His eyes blinked again—another wave of nausea traveled down to his stomach and made it do a back flip. Barry vomited again, more semi-solid chunks of food and acid. The pain was so great Barry clenched his eyes shut—

His stomach did another flip, and his body heaved, but nothing came out. Barry held his eyes open. He knelt there, arms soaked with vomit and acid, still holding the transfusion kit. He breathed. He coughed. His eyes watered. They screamed in pain. He didn't mean to blink, but it happened—

Barry heaved again. The impulse was so strong Barry's eyes clenched shut and his stomach flipped again and again. He clutched the kit and fell over to his side, heaving and choking.

"EVOLVE!   EVOLVE! EVOLVE! We are honored

to be present at this moment, when a new species takes over! A species who vows never to let this happen! We will never allow ourselves to forget why we are alive! We will make sure our bodies are full of life, as well as our souls, and we will never die a living death! We will never let our minds atrophy! We will never let our bodies die while we are still alive! WE WILL BE BETTER!"

Barry rolled around on the floor, heaving, clutching the kit so hard the plastic buckled.

"You almost had peace," said the voice of exploration. "If not for you, we would have missed this opportunity. We would have remained ignorant of our purpose. All of this is because of you, Barry. There's no need to fight it. Everything will be all right."

Barry clenched his teeth, held his eyes open and his stomach down. "NO! IT WON'T END LIKE THIS! SEEK THE LIGHT! SEEK THE LIGHT! SEEK THE LIGHT! SEEK! THE! LIIIIIIIIIGHT!"

Barry forced his neurons to form a new connection. He felt the floater-rigged neuron short circuit, and he regained control of his eyelids again. Barry blinked a few times without nausea. He rolled over and tore the cover off the needles on the kit.

Barry looked up and realized where he had rolled to. Center stage. His arms had become fractal eye floaters. His fingers had begun to merge together into vague web-like structures.

Barry's left eye watered. Profusely. Water gushed from it, obscuring his vision. Barry felt neurons being severed. He recognized them as neurons that inhibited pollen sensitivity. Without them, the eye switched to panic mode at the slightest speck of dust, and the hot air the audience kicked up blew enormous amounts into it.

His right eye followed. Barry clenched his eyes closed to try to hold off the flow, but the torrent was so great it pushed his eyelids open like an overwhelmed concrete dam. Barry held his hands in front of his eyes, trying to plug the leak. By now the torrent was so strong he couldn't hold his hands anywhere near his eyes.

"EVOLUTION IS HAPPENING IN FRONT OF US! WONDERFUL EVOLUTION! WONDERFUL FUTURE! BARRY DOUBLETAP IS THE FU-

TURE! EYE FLOATERS ARE THE FUTURE!"

Barry felt more neurons being cut and rewired. Ear wax production increased 200 fold and it clogged his ears and oozed out both sides of his head, shutting out all sound except for the voices of the four leaders.

"This is pointless, Barry," said the charismatic one. "We know your body better than you do. In another minute, you'll become the future."

Orgasms happened between Barry's toes. Hunger came from his teeth. His big toes felt lustful and his fingernails were sad. All of Barry's emotions pulled away from a central location and became spread out over his entire being. His bones craved ketchup and his penis began secreting enamel.

Barry screamed. He couldn't hear himself. Even his own internal voice was gone. His thoughts were strung out over his entire body, but Barry was still here. Yes, he was still here and he wasn't just going to slip away, not when he was so close.

Seek the light... Seek the light... Seek the light! SEEK! SEEK! SEEK! SEEEEEEEEEE—"EEEEEEEEEEEEEEK THE LIIIIIIIIIIIIIIIIIGHT!"

Barry's emotions and feelings and moods and thoughts sucked from various points all over his body and merged back into his head. His fingers responded, and Barry shoved the needles for blood transfusion into their proper places. He stuck the needles for lymph where they belonged, and the needles for bile and insulin.

The four leaders shouted at once.

"BARRY! NO!"

"YES!" Barry reached for the power switch.

His finger suddenly felt on fire. His eyes felt on fire. His whole body erupted into a flaming sensation. Barry struggled to move. Every time he even thought about using a motor neuron the pain became unbearable.

Neurons severed. Water erupted from his skin. They had cut the brain's discretionary center for when to sweat, so now the sweat glands secreted it constantly, without the safety valves. Sweat erupted in geysers. It blew holes in Barry's clothes, shredding them to pieces. Barry screamed in agony as his body locked down in pain and the audience screamed.

"WE SEE THE FUTURE! WE SEE IT! WE SEE THE FUTURE! WE ARE THE FUTURE! WE WELCOME IT! WE CRAVE A NEW LIFE! HUMANITY HAS CRAVED IT FOR GENERATIONS AND NOW WE WELCOME IT!"

Barry's finger hovered over the button. He strained and forced his finger to move, but it wouldn't. All he could feel was pain and sweat and water pouring from every microscopic opening in his pours. His tear ducts were gushing so fast they were raw.

More neurons were cut and reorganized. Barry saw the floaters swimming from his shoulders down his transparent skin to his arms. They attached the thick cable to his fingertips.

Barry blinked to ease the pain of the water erupting from his eyes. The spark of energy that would normally move his eyelids up and down instead traveled down this neuron and disappeared under all ten fingernails. They popped free and ejected. The pain signals traveled up these jerry-rigged neurons and directly to the pain center of his brain.

> "Just hold still!" shouted the voice of exploration. "This will be over soon!"

"No... I won't! I won't! I won't let it happen! I WON'T! I WILL SEEK THE LIGHT! I WILL SEEK IT! I WILL SEEK THE LIGHT! SEEK! SEEK! I WILL TAKE CONTROL! IT'S MY BODY! MY LIFE! MY LIFE! I'M IN CONTROL! CONTROL! CONTROL! MY LIFE! SEEK THE LIGHT! SEEK THE LIFE! SEEK LIFE! SEEK LIFE! I WILL SEEK LIFE!"

As Barry evolved, the audience chanted to counterbalance him.

"EVOLVE! EVOLVE! EVOLVE! EVOLVE! WE WELCOME IT! WE WILL EVOLVE! WE WILL EVOLVE!"

"SEEK THE LIFE! SEEK THE LIFE! SEEK THE LIFE! I AM ALIVE! I AM ALIVE! I AM NOT DEAD! HUMANITY IS NOT DEAD! WE WILL LEARN FROM OUR MISTAKES! WE WILL DELETE PLATFORM! WE SILL SIGN OUT! WE WILL UNPLUG! WE WILL CHOOSE OUR OWN MEALS! WE WILL MAKE OUR OWN CHOICES! WE WILL LIVE! I WILL SHOW THEM HOW TO LIVE AGAIN!"

Barry's mind zoomed around the planet 68 times, adjusted trajectory, and collided with his skull, sharing a full report with Barry's consciousness. It wasn't about weightloss. It never was—Barry could see that now. If only he had been smarter! If only he had taken a moment to ask why this was working, maybe he would have seen it sooner! He could have been so much more than just a conductor of weightloss! He could have been a conductor of humanity, showing human beings what they had been missing! Forcing their minds to come alive again, and their bodies along the way! He could have recharged the very spirit of humanity—their drive to imagine, to innovate, to explore, to choose their own meals and their own thoughts! He had wasted this opportunity, but now he understood! Now he saw just what he had and what it was supposed to mean! He wouldn't waste the opportunity again.

"GIVE ME ANOTHER CHANCE! GIVE! ME! ONE! MORE! CHANCE! I WILL SHOW THEM HOW TO LIVE! I WILL SEEK LIFE!"

He felt the new neurons severing. He had control of his fingers. Barry drilled the button.

"NO!" shouted the military voice.

"STOP RESISTING US!" screamed the voice of exploration.

The charismatic one: "IT'S TOO LATE TO SAVE THEM!"

The voice of reason: "WE ARE THE FUTURE!"

"Get out!"

Seconds passed. His body continued to erupt water and ear wax. Seconds turned into tens of seconds. Nothing was happening. The four leaders turned and looked through Barry's iris at the machine. They seemed just as puzzled as he was.

No movement through the tubes. Barry felt no transfusion occurring.

A solid minute passed. The audience continued to chant. Barry's body continued to shift from skin and bone to webby membrane. He felt his emotions dissipating along the whole of his fractal form. Barry's vision zoomed in on the logo just barely visible on the top of the machine through the vomit.

Ripauf: quality ideas meet cost-effective manufacturing.

Barry sighed. "Crap."

The four leaders turned around and faced Barry. Barry swore he saw them smile.

> "Thanks for giving us a chance to evolve," said the military voice. "Goodbye."

"No! No! I see it now! I SEE IT! GIVE ME ANOTHER CHANCE, PLEASE!"

The four leaders left Barry's eye and joined the others. Barry's arms let go of the machine. His fractal body kicked out the needles. The skin on the body wiped from opaque to transparent. His muscles joined with his skin. His bones melted and joined his body. His head disappeared. Barry's emotions spread out over his entire body. Each piece of his body contained the whole. His body became web-like, elongated, seeming to float in the air.

Barry was rising. The air had become the vitreous humor in which he drifted.

Seconds later, the audience fell silent. The slideshow ended. The audience morphed into fractal eye floaters. They rose into the air, level with Barry. Air currents pushed them together. They traded pieces with one another. Each part contained the whole of their experiences. In no time, everyone shared the same memories. Barry became the influencers who became the cameramen who became the slob from Delaware who became the single mother from Germany who became everyone else in the room.

The stream reached millions of viewers. Billions of eye floaters saw what they could become, and they achieved intelligence and evolved to join their brethren. The transformation was so gradual it was painless to the home viewers.

The floaters took to the streets. They interchanged parts with one another. Entire towns shared a collective identity. Entire cities became millions of fractal creatures, many parts making up a single whole, and each part comprised the single whole in itself.

The entire planet came together in this way. Every city in every country on every continent.

They didn't converse. They merely traded parts. The sum of knowledge existed worldwide. Barry's consciousness spread out over the whole, and yet it remained intact. It experienced the end result of his weightloss program. While it didn't regret the final result, part of it still wondered if things would have been different had a better man been given the opportunity to save humanity.

A new feeling rushed through the collective floater-consciousness.

Seek the light.

As one, the eye floaters gazed upward. They observed the movement of the sun, the winking of the stars, the planets and galaxies. They discerned shapes in the patterns of light and darkness and concluded that there must be more like them out there.

Quickly they grew tired of observing, and a new desire took over: to experience what they had once only been able to observe. Other spheres. They would seek them out.

February – July 2012
February – December 2023

Keep 'em coming, guys.

Barry needs a new pair of eyes.

About the Author

James L. Steele's eye floaters wrote EEF more than a decade before they released it. This gave them time to fine-tune the internal logic and remove material that just didn't work.

They have been published in various anthologies and magazines, including: *The Furry MEGAPACK®*, *Zooscape*, *Tall Tales with Short Cocks V.2*, *The Magazine of Bizarro Fiction*, *The Best of Bizarro V.1*, and *Cosmic Muse: Best of NewMyths Anthology V.4.*

Their novels include *Huvek*, and the six-volume *Archeons* series.

They live in Ohio, where they manipulate their human vessel into becoming a wine connoisseur while laughing at their existential crises.

DaydreamingInText.blogspot.com

@JLSteeleAuthor

www.ingramcontent.com/pod-product-compliance
Lightning Source LLC
Chambersburg PA
CBHW070343200726
48294CB00003B/762